TWILIT HORIZON:

Sentiments of the Seasons

*An Anthology of Edison Dizon's
Best Works*

With A Foreword And Introduction By:
JOMARI PANGILINAN

Written by
EDISON DIZON

Published by Poetry Planet Book Publishing House
Designed by Micaella Dizon
Edited and Compiled by Jomari Pangilinan

Please submit all reviews and comments or report errors to edisondizon@hotmail.com.

ISBN:

Hardbound-

Softbound-

Mobile/Kindle-

FOREWORD

"There is nothing to writing; all you do is sit down at a typewriter and bleed" – Ernest Hemingway. The author of the works in this book has indeed bled his way to success. Nothing stopped him from pouring his thoughts and emotions into written works of art. I have never seen writings more heartfelt that his.

An educator, a writer, an artist, a trainer, and a motivational speaker – Edison Dizon is a lot of things. He received his master's degree in education and professional degree in higher education studies from Concordia University in Canada. Recognitions such as "Classroom Superhero" and "Outstanding Teacher" were awarded to Edison as evidence of his excellence and dedication to the teaching profession. This multi-awarded educator and best-selling author is now a few steps away from obtaining his doctorate proving him to be a lifelong learner. He also had the chance to write articles and journals in the field of education both locally and internationally.

The writer began his passionate journey into literature as early as his teenage years. He started writing at the age of 17 when he was in college and has published nine books thus far namely: Shades of Seasons: Soulful Autumn; Shades of Seasons: Cold Dark Winter's Night; Shades of Seasons: Endless Spring; Shades of Seasons: Summertime Blues; Isang Tasa ng Tsaa Para Sa'yo: Tula at Prosa; The Voice Within My Soul; Tag-Ulan sa Kaarawan ni Juan: Dagli at Maikling Kwento; The Soul Sentiments: No Blames For This Pain and other Selected Poems; and The Soul Sentiments: Like Last Night Never Happened and other Selected Verses. Edison paved his way to adulthood through writing making his works relatable to every person who experienced becoming an adult.

Edison is an inspiration to many aspiring authors, me included. Considering that he is renowned as one of the greatest writers in his generation, he is a kind and generous mentor who exudes humility amid his excellence in the field. Opening doors to people and providing them opportunities to become better versions of themselves are some of the few things Edison has the ability to do effectively. He motivates people to try new ventures and to reach new heights by erasing the hesitations in their minds. According to him, there are a lot of people with exceptional potentials who only need a little push to realize that achieving success is within their grasps; Edison gave me that push and made me discover that I was fated to be a writer and to accomplish greatness.

This anthology is a collection of Edison's finest works in his current writing career. It consists of poetry and prose from his previously published books written solely for the purpose of seizing overflowing human emotions and experiences into sublime readings. This anthology covers different seasons that reflect different phases in a person's life: the melancholic fall, the biting cold of winter, the hopefulness of spring, and the warmth of summer. Every season is different for every person, and the writer made sure to portray those interpretations with a variety of literary pieces in the form of poems, verses, flash fictions, short stories, and essays.

People who stay under the sun for too long eventually get burnt; the night heals and provides rest. Most individuals hate the dark thinking that the dark may corrupt them. They say that the darkness is the absence of light; in my opinion, what's wrong with a little shade? Sometimes, we are destined to be lost in an unlit void in order for us to discover the path to light. Edison's work is not a children's book; it hits us with the reality. It consists of mental issues and traumas we didn't know we had; it covers sorrowful events in our lives; it depicts human pain and suffering; it conjures the feeling of loss and emptiness.

Every page is like a day in a person's life: you will never know what's next. In between the demise, we are reminded that life is good and still worth living; that no matter how damaged we are, we survive; that every person is capable of healing; that being lost in a maze doesn't mean you'll never make it out; and that no pain is permanent if you choose to love.

Every individual undergoes different emotional phases in both his young and adult life; Edison's writings capture those immense feelings and scattered experiences into literary masterpieces. Oddly, I have found solace in reading his work; every piece of literature triggers a sense of nostalgia that reminds me of moments in my life I have long forgotten: pain, joy, loss, hope, anger, and hate, yet his work makes me believe in love: love for family who we may eventually lose; love for time that we can never have enough of; love for oneself that we almost forget from day to day; romantic love that we have sought for, found, and lost; and lastly, love for solitude that proves that true peace starts from within.

—JOMARI PANGILINAN

February 01, 2021

San Matias, Santo Tomas

INTRODUCTION

Darkness is believed to be the absence of light. In the dark, everything is fair; everything is colorless. In the dark, everyone is on equal ground. The dark offers solace and healing.

The light, on the other hand, reveals our appearance; it exhibits ourtrue nature, our beauty, our hue, but it also reveals our differences, our flaws, our weaknesses.

What's wrong with a little shade every now and then? The light has been romanticized countless of times. The sun which produces light has symbolized so much: hope, brightness, fortune, heaven, godliness, etcetera; however, the dark has its own romance to offer.

The shadows bring us comfort; it dims our inhibitions in life and hides our feebleness. Being in a dark place is unavoidable for a person. We may have different reasons to resort to the dark, but it's common for anyone to seek shade when exposed too much to the sun.

One cannot help but fall in love with the night; it is indeed the time for rest and peace. The sky enchants us with its glitters, and the moon charms us with its glow. The night ends the day; it erases all the worries and grief we faced in the daytime and gives us the confidence that there will be another tomorrow waiting for us. Will it be a better tomorrow or not? No one knows.

Nonetheless, the dark offers its fair share of danger. People who get the taste of its comforts are enticed to succumb deeper into the abyss completely losing track of whence they came. The passage becomes murkier and leads the souls astray erasing the route back to light. The dark seduces us to a path going nowhere, a path to an endless void, a path to self-destruction and decay.

However you look at it, either having too much day or an endless Nyx entails trouble. Imagine a world without darkness; everything will be hot and scorching; similarly, a world without light will not let anything grow. A balance is required to survive; when there's light, there's darkness; when the sun sets, the moon rises.

Twilight – the faint glow of the sun below the horizon.

Whether it signals the rising of the sun or its setting, twilight marks the conclusion of a period and the birth of another. Twilight gives us hope that the end is only the beginning; it is the fine line between light and dark, between the seen and hidden, between day and night.

As humans, we must always look forward; we must strain our eyes to see beyond obstacles, to see farther than the eyes can see, to see past the insecurities. Life is a series of ups and downs; not because we're rock bottom, we're destined to stay down forever.

A human life is like the planet earth; it cycles. Along with the earth's changing seasons, one's life weathers many phases.

Our childhood is spring where flowers bloom just like our birth, just like how the world welcomed our delivery. The curiosity brought by our innocence offers us endless wonders that shine before our bright eyes. Our thirst for answers drives us to explore the world, appreciating all the beauty it has to offer.

Summer represents the years of our youth; it's warm and exciting. The adventures we went through and the challenges we conquered are instrumental to the path toward self-discovery. We get to test the waters and learn how to experiment in life just like how we experiment with different ice cream flavors. Summer allows us to enjoy life and its warmth; it also teaches us the value of consequences and how lack of preparation for the heat gives us sunburn afterward.

Adulting is our autumn. Most of our passions begin to fade as the leaves wither in fall. This is when reality hits us hard; it's the collapse of our youth. Similar to autumn's calm, our youth begins to die down as our wisdom begins to set in. Fall is the season of ripening and maturity; to a person, it's the time he learns from his mistakes. Fall signals that the last chapters of our lives are approaching, so we either prepare for it or it catches us off guard.

Winter: everything begins freeze. If only we could also freeze time, we would probably avoid the inevitable end. Snow brings forth cold, and the cold numbs our pains but inflicts us with a different kind of pain. The biting cold can cause our hearts unable to feel, and feeling nothing is the worst feeling of all. When our hearts are rendered frozen, it's just a matter of time before it shatters completely making it impossible to mend.

Thawing out a frozen heart is a difficult task. Some think that we need others to melt our hearts for us; however, no matter how many torches and bonfires people light for us, if we don't step out of winter, we'll remain frozen.

As humans, we deserve to end our seasons with a warm heart with no regrets. Learn how to be your own flame amidst the wintry spectacle of life.

Learn how to step out of the cold to have the sun shine its radiance onto your being. Learn to illuminate your own way through a dark void and cast your own shadow in a bright and blinding plane. Learn to be your own dark in the day and your own light in the night. Learn to be twilight.

To the readers:

Wherever you are and whatever you do, I know you're starting to feel it, too. Our younger selves have taken so many opportunities for granted: moments we could have spent learning a skill, moments we could have used to rest, and moments we could have used to love rather than hate. We're wishing clandestinely that we could turn it all back, but time hasn't been kind to us. There are no pauses nor rewinds to relive the best days of our lives; there are no nexts nor fast forwards to skip the bitterness and struggles life has thrown at us. All we can do is sit back and witness the world changing before our eyes and hope for the best, hope for a brighter future for our kids, and hope for a gentle death without holding regrets.

"The past is the beginning of the beginning and all that
is and has been is but the twilight of the dawn."
—H.G Wells

CONTENTS

Soulful
Autumn

"Every leaf speaks bliss to me,
fluttering from the autumn tree"
—Emily Brontë

AN HOUR TO REMEMBER

Melancholy has eaten me up.
Tick-tock, my time is about to end.
I let out several coughs.
Wrapped around my warmest blanket.
Asking who would the angels send.

Skin so pale like the sky about to rain.
Every single move I make corresponds to severe pain.
Tears fall down from my cheeks.
Wondering how long I will be sick.

I tried to keep my heads up; I know I need to fight.
And I hope my body will do the same.
Yet I cannot handle this alone, I cannot hold on tight.
Too bad I need to wait for my time to came.

My wish for them is to stay in the midst of joy.
Although I will not be around for every moment to enjoy.
How thankful I am to experience the gist of life.

Goodbye, the worst word to utter which stabs me by a knife.

UNPREDICTABLY INEVITABLE

It's terrifying to think about leaving the world when we're yet to be ready. To see the ending that we wished we could postpone for a little while because our heart's still into prepared to live the life we built so many plans in the future with. In an instant, we get to think about all the things we did in the past. All the chances we allowed to slip our grasp because we thought we have so many times in the future to do it. We tend to look back to all weaknesses we never acknowledged because we didn't want to take things seriously yet.

But when you woke up and realized that your time was limited, when you have come to realize that you could no longer seize the moment, and when you tend to engross the sad truth that tomorrow is never guaranteed, we suddenly found ourselves wanting to stop the world from revolving. We tried to stop the morning from slowly turning into nights. We suddenly want to hold the hands of the clock and freeze everything that surrounds us. We want to change things for the better, hoping we still have time, hoping we're still facing a thriving life instead of death.

Just as much as we want to halt the waves from moving forward, or stop the rains from pouring, we knew that we couldn't. Life, after all, was unpredictable, and death has always been inevitable. Sometimes, we were left with no choice.

TIME'S UP

We don't know how far life would go.
Have we enjoyed the passing moment as we grow?
Have we seen the purpose that life tries to show?
Or have we been wasting our time and preferring
not to know?

It sometimes scares us to think about the end.
We don't know when we will break after we bend.
We have so many scars that we never truly mend.
And we have so many tears we never entirely shed.

Our fate turned out to be something we can't read.
We thought we have so many wonderful chapters
ahead.
But suddenly we're running out of time, that's what
they said.
And we will leave the world with nothing but
memories to dread.

To face life with the fear of death,
We sip through the smell of mornings through our
breath.

We stayed out of the things that represent depth
Because we thought we still have time that's on full length.

We all worry about death because we never felt so alive.
We all wake up every morning just to survive.
Death, after all, felt like a stab at the back with hundred knives,
Because life's too short, we don't know when our time will arrive.

One day soon, we will vanish and be totally gone.
So we should seek for purpose, like the sun at dawn.
We should stop worrying about the past that can't be drawn.
And be thankful that we are here for a reason since the day we were born.

WHAT IS BEAUTY?

I grew tired of understanding people's definition of pretty.

It's too broad, and they only prefer to define the surface. They call it beauty when things are aligned so well, when lips are pouted, when the body appeared like an hourglass, when eyes are round and rare, when the nose is pointed, and when the skin is fair. I grew tired of hearing all these standards that people associate to beauty. It's like setting the bars high for society.

It's too frustrating because it's unfair. It's unfair because beauty is not something that should only settle on superficial things. All my life, I knew beauty means the goodness of the heart. I knew it is the words you spurt out, and they consist of wisdom. Beauty means having a passion for pushing through despite how hard life might be. It is inspiring people, helping them emerge from their different versions of drowning. I knew beauty as knowing their real purpose and having a sincere heart to see and accept one's imperfections.

And I will continue to live unapologetically for the things that I am and for the features that I am not. I look at myself in front of the mirror, and I know that I am someone who's stitched with flaws and errors. I take my imperfect self imperfectly because I have no one to prove myself to. I am here to show everyone that having a good heart means beautiful. I will get tired of listening to how the world set up their own criteria of beauty. But I will never get tired loving myself —for who I am and for who I will become.

TIED TILL THE END OF TIME

Under the shining stars and in the midst of the
dark.
A lady walks so demure.
Creating a silhouette which is fascinating for sure.
Around her is such a giant spark.

Walking right towards her, I am truly favored.
To have her as my other half seem impossible.
Her face is so perfectly tailored.
Also having the voice so soft and far from being
horrible.

Such moments like this I don't want to end.
Magical it is to be with the likes of her.
As I caresses her skin that is fair.
Along with the promise, what we have, I will always
defend.

Even when we hit the sixties .
Waltzing across the room like there's no tomorrow.
I will still look at her as the lady who shines like a
pixie.
Who is special and had erased all my sorrow.

ESCAPE

Let's go on a trip.

Let's see where these pathways head to. Let's disconnect from the topsy-turvy world for a while and get lost to a place nobody knows about. Let's escape the reality and bury some footsteps on white sands where nights give us promising sparks from the stars. Let's look forward to spending the night listening to the music of waves and the chirps of birds as they head to their homes. Let's talk about the good and bad things that happened to our lives and unload our hearts from its weight by allowing the November wind to shoo it away

Let's go on a trip.

Let's take as many pictures as we can with greens and browns blending perfection on the background. Let's take as many photos where nature gives us the best freebie of its immeasurable beauty. Let's hold each other's hand as we walk in between wild trees; let's take the most remarkable trek that we could. Let's explore the unknown and travel to places we've never been. Let's climb the tallest mountains and savor the victory of reaching the apex with determination

Let's go on a trip.

Let's enjoy every moment that we could get away from everyone. We will look down on paper houses when we reach the top of the world, and we will stare endlessly to the stars during the night. We will fall in love over and over again without knowing how and when to stop.

Let's go on a trip.

Just the thought of walking away from this messy place gives me the thrill and hope. Perhaps, that's the best thing about nature. It gives us a go-to place when we want to get lost for a little while.

CONCEALED BEAUTY

And she had always been the prettiest,
Her hair flows freely against the wind,
To be her was everyone's wish.
And sitting next to her would make one shrink.

She has a pretty laugh and the softest skin.
Everyone adores her; everyone falls for her grin.
Her body was so thin; she was indeed slim.
But behind her beauty, something hides within.

As everyone fell for her beautiful smile,
And how she's been adored by her lifestyle.
She knew her beauty from the inside won't transpire.
Because she was unhappy, and it's been a while.

Behind her optimism and pretty face,
She somehow goes through an ugly phase.
But she wanted to remain brave in her own ways.
She tried to conceal her weakness and preferred to stay.

Her beauty remains, but she never called it grace.

While everyone's craving since she's someone worth the chase

She silently smiles, knowing it's not easy to be in her place.

Nobody sees the pain that pours when it rains.

She has the perfect body, all everything you could ask for.

Her emptiness felt too much —sadness as she called.

That she knew nobody would dare to fall.

AND just because she's beautiful doesn't mean she has it all.

THE IRONY OF TIME

Time is mischievous. It's an irony. Sometimes, when you feel like you're enjoying the moment, time starts running so fast. Everything appears to shorten. When you're happy, the world starts spinning rapidly. But when you're sad, everything starts to feel like time begins moving sluggishly. Time becomes a traitor that prolongs your agony. It starts ticking like forever and the world stops from revolving.

Maybe that's why my misery began weighing heftier than my happiness because time made me realize that I spent more of my attention savoring the pain. I remember the ache because it soothes within my flesh. I remember the chaos because I start counting for seconds to turn into minutes. It was so odd how the world never corresponded to the workings of my heart.

But despite how time crawled in aguish with me, I also believe that all of my storms will turn into light rains if I believe in the ironies of time. I will keep holding on to the belief that time will heal me. It may be ironic but I hope soon it will help me understand the ugly phases I've been through.

The purpose of time has always been unpredictable, always indistinct. You don't know if it will help you or it will drown you; you don't know if it will make you or break you, but whatever it may be, I hope time ticks because there's a reason behind. Good or bad, I know it's all because of fate.

For now, I will be cautious. I will keep steering. I will keep healing.

MOTHER CRYING FOR MIRACLES

Creatures battling for food and living.
Without having the idea of the hindrances they are having.
Loud roars from the horizon can be heard.
It is either because they are contented or scared.

Song birds that used to calm the ears of anybody.
Tend to hide away from the people that seem shady.
Humans who used to partner with nature.
Act to destroy the environment now for sure.

How long will the awakening be?
Do we need to hear Mother Nature cry and see?
Trees that used to shade us from beaming sunlight.
Animals which are slowly being out of sight.

And the deep rivers whisper for help.
"Please, I cannot handle this by myself"
The world needs a relaxation.
Kindly be watchful of your environmental decision.

THE ONE THAT GOT AWAY

She still thinks of him, her first love. She still thinks about the time they have lost because they were still too young to understand love. She still thinks about what might have happened if she learned to stand on solid ground and chose him — no matter how the world became so against them. She still thinks of him because he is her one true love and nothing in this world could make her fall in love the same way he did. She wonders if they'll end up happy because letting him go only made her miserable as she closed all her doors for someone new. She locked herself in a room where her regrets hanged on the walls. She hated how she never listened to her heart. She hated herself for not combating the expectations that were asked to her by the world to memorize. She hated herself for not knowing what her future would be like if only she was stronger and more firm to her decisions.

She hated the world for not giving her the person who will make her the happiest. She hated how innocent she was and not believing in him that they will face all odds together.

Perhaps, she will spend the rest of her life regretting the decisions she made because it left her a scar — a scar that will stay with her forever no matter how much she tried to conceal it. That's the power of love; it takes over your entire system. That's how capable it is to build your world and destroy it in just a matter of a minute. That's the thing about regrets; it stops you from seeing the world from a better angle.

SOLITUDE COMES FOR FREE

The sun peeks outside my window.
The leaves started to turn dry yellow.
The November breeze gave my cheeks a cold blow.
As I wished, there's winter here so I could experience snow.

The waves of the ocean have always been angry.
I would sit on the shore to where my feet I desire to bury.
I am feeling the soft grains that are too white and tiny.
This is indeed the gift of nature that's too heavenly.

The sun would slowly sulk; it's time to set.
I would get up with my feet that are still too salty wet.
The sky will turn into pastels, like an orange and light red.
A peaceful afternoon with silence is time well spent.

The trees sang along with the birds' chirps.
It was soothing, that's all I heard.

It gave me the solitude that I always search.
And it sounded exactly like happiness that surged.

The nights hold my secrets and scars.
I will never get tired of looking at all these blinking stars,
As I get lost to its magnificent sparks.
Through them, I learned to love my ugly past.

The world holds such wonders.
I swear I will never get tired to wander.
Looking through the ocean's calmness, I knew I could ponder,
It heals almost all wounds to make me better.

LIFE'S REAL MEANING

I want to spend the rest of my life chasing life's real meaning. I want to unleash the parts of me that are looking for belongingness. I want to explore as many places as possible if that would mean seeing where I truly belong —if that would mean realizing solitude is the best cure from this clamorous world. I want to see where my passion will take me.

I want to spend the rest of my life chasing life's real meaning. I want to know how I will be able to conquer all of my insecurities until I am able to wash me off and come out clean and brave. I want to see where my perseverance will take me, and when I am able to create a place where I can unload all of my frustrations away.

I want to spend the rest of my life chasing life's real meaning. I want to know when I will able to step up and help others through my words. I want to witness how my poetry will break all their walls and help them soar. I want to know when I will be heal from the wounds and watch it turn into scars.

    I understand that life is not just about sunrise constantly greeting you freestanding from my window first thing in the morning, sometimes the rain is the first thing I'll get to wake up to. It's not always about summer the whole year and supposes that there'll be no storm to drop by to create casualty. And I know there'll be another living proof of how it feels dealing with relentless rains while having no vision of hope. I learned that life is an exhausting trek, but it will always be a good experience. It's still worth the bend so that I won't break. It's always worth trying —always worth conquering.

ETERNAL AFFECTION

She walks right up to me.
Telling me not to waste any opportunity.
Like an alarm, he told me to move my body.
Someone's needs to get ready.

Sure, I have a lot to go through.
Definitely would not mind being in a crew
Tick-tock, I hear that stupid clock.
Shining doors are ought to be locked.

I need to move fast.
Don't want to see everything slowly turning into dust.
No matter how difficult it is.
Him and her did not mind targeting my cheeks for a kiss.

Great! They said they will be here until the end of time.
Precious with you, Ma and Pa cannot be paid by a single dime.
Oh clock! Hang on! Stop for a bit!

These are the times; I treasure most without having in mind the word, "quit".

LUCKY

I had always been fortunate that I get to wake up every morning with a mission. It's rewarding to realize that I have a drive and that I am able to be part of an organization that hones me to be better every single day. I know not everyone has the chance to find work they could truly enjoy, that working doesn't feel like a job at all. And I am thankful because I get to see myself wanting to spend my day dealing with the routine work I'll never get tired of doing.

So I am determined to learn because I know it will help me grow. I am keen to analyze the errors in my code, so I could transform it into my asset someday. I will keep bringing myself to new visions that will add up to my inspirations. All these graces are the reasons why I am thankful for myself for still trying, for never allowing one failure to stop me from reaching for the clouds. This is the reason why I am in love with life. Life perhaps was never fair at all. Everything pays off when you give yourself the chance to try.

DETESTING MY FLAWS

Today, I stood up browsing the entire me.
What a shame I should be.
Why do I have to be in the dark before I see?
That this misery is for eternity.

I'm just typical filled with imperfections, that's true.
Which is why I'm constantly feeling blue.
Can you tell me why? Someone give me a clue.
It's been haunting me; it's inside me, sticking with me like glue.

Someone please help me forget.
This heavy pain gnawing now, the burden of regret.
I have been longing for the happiness I could not get.
I just wish my old self is someone I never met.

Actions that sucked up all my dignity.
As I walk alone in this city.
Yes, I understand I'm just a pity.
Maybe someday someone will walk right up to me.

And will not see me as someone who is completely dirty.

WORTH REMEMBERING

Sundays meant taking a break. We will ride in a rustic car and go straight to the beach. Grills and hotdogs skewered so temptingly, and the aroma has always been teasing. We will run to the shore and taunt the waves. I will build sandcastles under the blazing sun. I will hear my mother call my name from afar. The smile on her face always appears more apparent under the sun.

I will rush and take a seat on my father's lap. As I listen to their conversation which I barely understand. I barely finished half of my food on the plate since excitement always win. I will talk to Mama using my soft voice. I will ask if I could go back to finish my wind castle. She will tell me to wait for a little while because I don't have someone to look over.

I will sit on one side of the cottage, staring with astonishment at the kids playing everywhere. Their giggles put a smile on my face, and my feet have been so desperate to take a step. We will swim on the shallows, and Papa will carry me on his back. I remember the splashes of water and tanned skin. I will remember happiness through the look of everyone's face, and I agreed I had the best childhood tale.

We hopped in the car as I take one final look at that beautiful place. I will miss the clamor and strangers. Exhaustion started to soothe in on my system for all I knew, and we're heading home. I took one last look as the engine started. Slowly, the wooden cottage, the bluish sea, and the pastel sky turning miniature in my sight. I faced forward with a frown on my face, then father smiled at me, "we will be back again someday."

HAUNTED

There are nights when I am still haunted.
The echoes still sounded so vivid.
The words on the walls, they're still painted.
Regrets stayed with me as expected.

I didn't know I am stranded as I waited.
For the chances that I pathetically wasted.
Perhaps, I lost it all, and it will never be granted.
I will stay here next to all these lost probabilities
that I once doubted.

I sometimes wonder why I am still having troubles,
I wished I never allowed my desires to turn into
bubbles,
I wished I fought harder on these battles.
And survive everything that stood as hurdles.

Now I have to face all these sleepless nights.
Moments where I am towered by my frights,
I wished I gave myself a good try to fight.
And make all these panoramic opportunities turn
blatant and right.

I'll keep on wondering when it will all fade.

Remorse and sadness for the hopeful ventures I never take.

I never took the initiative, and I permitted for regrets to outweigh.

Maybe I was just too afraid of what will come if I failed,

I wish one day I will be able to overcome.

I hope my daylight will soon turn more golden.

I hope my prayers will soon happen.

And I will be able to forget how my weakness left me broken.

HOME

You, above anyone else, became the only person who gave me the freedom to be my crazy self with and eradicate the fear of judgment at all. You gave me that kind of comfort that taught me how to actually peak out from my box of concerns and trust the world outside because I am better than my worries and fears. You've been so open with me with your issues and that's when you showed me my worth because you trusted me enough, and that alone made me realize that you are truly different from the rest. You suddenly became my comfort zone; a person who could make me feel safe when I am still in the process of discovering myself. You are that someone who assured me that I will have someone I could run to no matter what the weather is. I know I have someone who will listen to me when all ever received from everyone else is uninterested shrugs. You are that someone who won't judge my past, who will see the story behind my past and will understand all the stains I left on my skin from all the wrong decisions that I have made.

I hope that unlike the rest, the connection that we have will last longer than it should. I believe that we don't share superficial memories just to be forgotten over time. I trusted us way too much that not even distance and physical absence could stand in between. Instead, we are made of both storms and sunshine that stood the test of time. Always remember that you will have me in ways that you wanted me to be. Any season and whatever reason it may be. I hope you will keep me that way too. I hope I mean the same way to you too.

THROUGH UPS AND DOWNS

And I had always told you that the world has always
been lucky to have you,
You're that one friend who's gentle in everything
that you do.
You always made me happy and always changed
what made us blue,
You're the best friend that I have dressed in colors
as perfect as sunset's hue.

I am so blessed to have a friend, and in my heart,
you took the greatest part.
Through our friendship, I realized that you have the
sincerest heart.
You speak with respect, like poems aligned with
rhythm and art.
You always give your all, always standing guard
right from the start.

You're more than what we wished for; you're more
than enough.
You always give what you have, always sharing until
you're left with half.

You have a friend in me who will stay even when the road gets rough.
You're the best for me, and you are deserving of love.

You had always been willing to run, may it be far or near.
And for our friendship, I swear I will conquer my fear.
Because of you, everything started to show up clear.
And that's why everybody wants you around— wants you here.

I will always trust you because there's nothing to hide.
You had always been real, and through old age, I want you to stay on my side.
You say the best phrases until all wrongs began sounding right.
They all lead to something; your words became my guide.

You're the best of everything, the sunshine when the rain is bleak.

You gave optimism, mending everything that used to break.

You gave such vibes that unite, a home is what you create.

You always teach my heart how to love until it learns to forget about hate.

WORTH EVERYTHING

They say love is what makes the world go round but sometimes I wonder what happens to love after the other decides to take the initiative of leaving first.

Somehow, it's hard to admit that one person remains on the same ground while the other decides to stay. It's really hard falling for someone knowing you won't get that smooth landing at all but somehow, that's what unconditional love is all about, right? Always wanting to love the other despite knowing you won't receive the same thing in return. I guess loving someone who refused to love you back was the toughest thing you wanted to scrape off from your heart. Loving that someone makes things so much harder than you thought it could be. But love somehow makes us all feel alive. Then you start to remember how it all began. It's was a mixture of confusion and never-ending uncertainties.

Maybe this time, you learn that love will always have its power over you. Your heart and mind will never agree with each other, and you'll find yourself constantly choosing that person over and over again under any circumstances. You wanted to let that person know that you will always be here, hoping your heart made the rightest choice and you hope both of you will make up to the time and chances that you've lost. You hope that someday it'll be your time; that both of you will be brave enough to fight for the feelings that felt so right and real; and that we should never let it slip away. You keep hoping that person will always remember that you're there and will wait because you know everything is worth it. When it comes to that person, every heartache you've been through is worth it.

Cold Dark Winter's Night

"Melancholy were the sounds on a winter's night"
—Virginia Woolf

THE MURDER

Blood spattered on the floor.
The crime happened between midnight and four.
Everything was closed, —all windows and door.
It was all planned when everyone's deep at snore.

The morning came, the house was silent.
The neighbors felt that within the house, there's a different climate.
They soon called the cops; the street is echoed with sirens.
The body of a dead young woman broke the silence.

Rumors fly, everyone started whispering.
All ears that day were made for listening.
Police and winesses even began bickering.
The evil husband —everyone knew this day was coming.

The hunt for his whereabouts began.
He escaped after he succeeded in his plan.
The experts tracked down, he was an evil man.

The family sought justice and searched for places he might have ran.

After a few more days, he was found hiding in a secluded town.
He looked depressed, tired, and drown.
He didn't resist, regret through his words became the clear sound.
He didn't mean what he did, he said to everyone around.

He killed her for temporary anger and jealousy,
He killed her because of her infidelity.
But it doesn't justify why he had to kill her helplessly.
So he's facing life in prison forever —regrettably.

LOSING AND BREAKING

When you grew so attached to someone, you stopped imagining what your life would look like with someone else. Everything started to fade into the background, and that person became the only radiant color you want to spend the rest of yourself staring at.

I love you and that goes without saying and maybe that's why losing you hurts. I love you to the point that I saw my future in you. I saw a family that I wanted to take care of in you. I imagine us growing old together and conquering the world with our love. I imagined you being with me for the rest of my life. I imagine us building our dreams together and sharing success. It has always been the life that I carved in my head, with just me, you, and to the family that we will create. A family that I wanted to protect against everything and everyone.

But right now, it seemed like all of them crashed right in front of me and all I could ever do was watch them break me. All I could ever do was watch them stop me from doing the things I love. They reminded me about the pain of losing you — the kind of loss that I know time could no longer bring back. The kind of loss that will never heal from no matter how much I try. No matter what I will do, there's no way possible to pull you back and be here —physically present. No matter what happens, you will always be this ache that I will keep crying from, the scar I will keep scratching. You will always be the only irreplaceable memory that my heart will forever remember. It still aches for you because it still loves you and always will be.

Even after a year of not having you here, I never stopped loving you.

My heart only recognizes you yet I knew I keep losing you.

I keep losing us.

RUINED

For a moment, my entire hopes crumbled in front of me, and no matter how much I wanted to pick them up piece by piece, I lost all my strength. After all, nothing came right, everything was a plain blur and I knew deep within that you're the only name I wanted to hear, the only person I wanted to be with, the only wish I want to be granted, and the prayer I wanted to be heard. But we were a hopeless case. I realized that it's no longer just me and my feelings, it's no longer about me saving what we almost lost and our possibilities because sadly, there was never even a chance.

I wanted to let you know that the pain was still sharp and I am still astray. I still don't know where I am going to after you left me. I don't know why I have to go through this and why pain never ceases to stop burning.

I miss you so bad that I could never have the same sound of my laughter with someone else. I wanted to regain what I lost that I wished someone else could give me but I was wrong. The more I met so many people the more I realized that they can't replace the vacancy that you left in me. You're the only hand that my body wanted to feel the touch with. You're the only person who could mend me. If only I could be selfish but I know I can't be this harsh and mean to ruin you although I knew that your mistakes ruined us.

If only I could be so selfish and tell you this is where you belong —here with me.

Maybe you became my favorite pain.

THEIR ENDING ENDED US

Sometimes, I wonder why things have to end and that most of us never knew that it was it.

I wonder if people leaving us planned it way too long ago that once they end everything in front of us, they walk away straightly with no turning backs. It was like they envisioned how that ending would look like, what words will be said and heard, and how it will work perfectly for them.

And I wonder if they think about the wreckage that they left. I wonder if they think about how we will be able to cope with the pain they left. I wonder if they get the chance to see us start again or if we were just left there, sprawling on the same wooden floor thinking about so many things and hating the endings that they left for us to deal with.

Do they feel guilty for not giving us another chance to be better for them? Do they feel relieved the moment they detached from our grip and begin their life differently with someone else? Do they still think about us, about the aftermath and resonances of their goodbyes?

Do they still think about us? Are they even worried that maybe we still don't understand why they have to go? Maybe they knew where to go after and sadly, we just got stuck for ages wondering about why we can't go on. Their words of endings somehow ended our happiness forever.

FAILURE ALLERGY

What shall I do when I feel like I am constantly making errors? What shall I do when I feel like I am not doing things right at all? What shall I do to stop myself from creating failures after failures after failures?

I am sick of giving my best. I am tired of telling everyone that I am good at everything. I am sick of showing to them that I never get weak. I am tired of always reaching for the top places, for the stars, for the expectations, and for their demands. It's like I am inside a room where all I could hear were their scripted pressure to let me do this and that as they anticipated for me to keep up with my composure and say no complaints at all. I am tired of standing way up high; when in reality, I wanted to sprawl on the floor and tell them that I was and will never be perfect.

People became too allergic to failures they trained people to be perfect. They put up labels and expect that we could all catch up to the responsibilities given to us. People are so disgusted with failures that people who committed it unintentionally were treated like another trash that needs to be replaced afterward.

Somehow, being a failure is terrifying. It's too much demand and too high to grab with both hands. Somehow, I hated myself for always obeying when I knew I have to endure greater pain and face greater consequences.

Perhaps, we all wished not to become another disappointment.

We all failed from not becoming a failure after all.

THE TANGIBLE PROBLEM

One of the things that I wasn't sure of any more about living is either I have to face the problem because I had no choice, or it was me who was really the problem here. I don't know if the purpose of my existence is to make me realize that there are so many things I was incapable of doing. It stopped me from stepping out of my comfort zone and prisoned my dreams along with dead encouragements.

For so long, I felt like I was a burden on someone's shoulder. It's like I was a hurricane, only made to destruct the things they built because I was just another mistake the broke down everything they started. A kind of burden that was too heavy and tiring to bring with. So they always leave me when they get a chance. And maybe that's why every time I looked at myself in the mirror, I could no longer determine which part of me was happy. Which part of me still believes in me. It was like happiness was drained off from my system; courage became another foreign language I don't understand, and I was surrounded by hopeless gloomy clouds. People blamed me for raining hard on their parade.

It was like I did nothing right, and I was just walking mistake breaking everything that comes along my way.

LIVING IN DESPAIR

I wonder why I have to go through all of these.
I didn't know who to please.
It seems like nobody agrees.
My mistakes are what the world sees.

I didn't know why all doors are locked.
The sunrise from my window is also blocked.
Everybody forgot how to knock.
Maybe I am no longer in their hearts.

Maybe for them, I have no cost.
In their minds, I never crossed.
I am just their version of the exhaust.
Maybe that's why I constantly feel lost.

To them I no longer have worth.
I feel like I have no safe place here on earth.
I am just wandering back and forth.
I am a story they pretended they never heard.

I mastered the art of concealing my hurt.
Nobody sees the scars I hid underneath my shirt.

My heart after all somehow felt like a desert.

All they see is my emptiness, my errors, and my dearth.

Somehow they didn't care.

I was just another invisible thing there.

A hollow chest that needs repair.

A tired body living in sorrow and despair.

ANEW

As days turned to months, I learned to slowly reconnect to the broken lines that I drew. There, I started to recognize why it was so easy for me to get hurt and why I was stranded on over feeling heartaches. All of these questions why I could comfort in being disconnected from everyone. I started gathering all these little reasons until I learned to open myself toward accepting who I was.

In there, I learned how to embrace change. I slowly discovered how to inhibit my struggles by acknowledging them and knowing that the only way to get rid of them is to welcome optimism. Gradually, I found new paths that would stop redirecting me to sadness. I learned to pave my way toward new habits and new routines. I engaged myself in exercise to uplift my mood, to reduce the time I was supposed to spend on overthinking. I started to become more concerned about my mental well-being and decided to prioritize myself. It was not an easy phase that I went through, but I endured all passing days and motivated myself enough until I managed to pluck up courage, especially in tough times. More so, I am confident to say that I surpassed that darkest moment of my life. I learned how to survive by believing that I can. So I moved forward even up until now. My depression reminded me of how brave I understood that life is imperfect, but I also knew that there's a possibility of moving forward and starting new again.

UNEXPECTED

It was Sunday, and I thought it was a calm peaceful day. I thought it was just an ordinary day along with my church dress, flat sandals, and never-fading gold necklace Mom gave me. I convinced myself to have a quick walk in the park before going home. I wanted to feel a bit of air and savor the rest of the time away from hectic schedules and unforeseen obligations that would eat the rest of the serenity of the day. I was walking, had a pick of chips, and a sip of cold soft drink.

I sat on a bench almost away from people, yet too close to see what happens to the busy street. The cars were speeding, the tires were screeching, and the sun was blazing. But then, there the sudden surprised noise intensified. The people were panicking, picking up phones, and trying to call for someone. It looked like it was in an emergency. I gathered my senses and decided to take my steps closer to it. People were encircling. Everyone is murmuring, and I was surprised to see an unconscious body lying on the floor. By the looks of it, I wonder if he's still alive. His chest wasn't listing. He was quite familiar, probably someone I came across with.

Sirens started sounding near; people were asked to give enough space. Everyone was in awe of the collision. Somehow, I realized none of us knew something that would happen. That's why it was an accident. We don't know which road will remain safe and which road will tell us it's the final destination.

Somehow, tragedy transpires the least we expected it.

Sometimes, it just happens.

MAKER AND BREAKER

Love has always been so strong that a single sentence will stand insufficient to support it. What is it that we know about love by the way? Love's more like a favorite book of yours. It becomes your favorite because it sent you many highs and lows. It gives you maximal affirmation of what you feel. It provides an overview of how great love can surmount. That's undefined. You see, love is more like an open sea that is seething.

Too deep to dive yet too soft if we know how to sway along with its waves. Love was pretty exciting yet too dangerous to try as well. It's too mysterious that no matter how much we try to plummet what's in there, it'll never be enough. There's always something that would break us, something that would tear us, or something that would puzzle us into whole again; however, we don't know what's down there.

Heartbreak is the scariest con of loving. Heartbreak is a dangerous feeling that we will experience when the right person suddenly turns out to be the total opposites. We love as it'll last forever; we give everything we have within because we thought we'll receive the same amount if we try harder. We love as we see ourselves in the future of that someone, only to watch everything fall rapidly on the ground and was too damaged to reassemble.

Love will hurt you in the cruelest way it could especially if you mishandled yourself along the process and when you ended up loving the wrong one.

Love is a maker and a breaker.

Both safety and danger.

PEOPLE

People are scary. They are either a reason why one failed to surpass a tragedy or the reason why it happened in the first place. People tend to objectify their rights by following what seems to be favorable to them. They always wants you to live in their scripts and tell you how you should run your life that would only accord to their wants and needs. They turn us into puppets whose strings we manipulated. These wrong people who did nothing right but to show to you how you should follow their steps for you not to get lost only to realize they are leading to you to wrong dark places.

People ended up sabotaging someone's day in the worst way possible, making it as tragic as they could. Making it too hopeless to endure. Manipulation, insecurities, wrath, greed, and risen pride become some of the factors why people tend to control the lives of others. They eliminate empathy as if they could play god anytime they want. They hold someone on the throat to threaten them. They brag their achievements so those who have nothing yet will remain in the same place and stop aiming for the stars at night. They tell stories of how they bloomed so others will wither. It's desperately taking advantage of what you could use. Desperation for power leads to clutching the last resort of scheming a tragic providence to end the collision, where every little detail is swept under the carpet and left no traces.

All aims to leave a mark in this world.

I hope everyone gets to be remembered for the better not as someone's other tragic history.

UNSEEN GHOST

As I look around,
My knees were shaking as I stood on the ground.
There's something I heard not too loud,
An inaudible sound.

I started to run down the stairs, fear still surrounds.
It swamps my chest, it made me feel drowned.
I sense something that cannot be found.
A lingering ghost I guess, it made my heart pound.

The door slowly creaks open.
My feet suddenly turned a little frozen.
There was a motion that I notice.
I could feel my entire system sink at my lowest.

I knew. I am sure that I am alone at home,
But I have these weird feelings that sometimes
roam.
It gives me chills because it was just me alone.
But I guess someone decided to accompany me —
the unknown.

I went back to the room, jumped on my bed.

I prayed harder than I did instead,

I told myself I should never be afraid of the dead.

Although my fears invaded my head,

I turned the lights on and forced myself to sleep.

I waited for mornings to come to sweep away the creep.

Although I feel that somewhere out there, someone sneak.

I closed my eyes tightly and waited for the sun to peek.

DO THE SAME

I sat there for a while thinking about the pain I still carry. I think about the weight on my shoulders and everything that I have to bring with me anywhere I go. I think about how it invades my peace, how it takes away my happiness, and how it stops me from seeing things in a radiant sight. I think about how empty my heart feels and watch how this pain takes one step at a time to reside inside my chest.

Somehow, I don't understand why I have to get this ache when all I ever did was love, give what I am capable of giving, and do the things that would put them in their comfortable places. I never asked anything in return but only for them to remain true.

Maybe that's why I am feeling this burden because I thought they were true to me. I thought they are worth my trust. I thought they were different from the rest. I called them my friends. I treated them as my family. I gave them half of me. I showed them my fragility. I thought everything's taken with value, but I drank my own poison because, after all, they were these people I never imagined them to be.

They hurt me, and the pain is something that I can't erase even if I cry hard, even if I sleep longer, and even if I try to force myself to forget. It never fades and I need to do something. I thought I could. I thought I should. I thought I'll be okay if I hurt them the way they hurt me.

ENDING THIS PAIN

My heart has gone cold, distant, and hopeless.

Sometimes, my sadness looks like the moon in the vast night sky, sometimes I am surrounded by darkness, everything was jet-black, I was pretending I could stand alone and shine, but I am uglier up close. I have so many craters I refused to call as scars. I have so many valid reasons for this loneliness, for this emptiness, and for this never-ending self-blames.

Sometimes, my sadness looks like a blank promise, an unclear undertaking. It looks like my failures that never really left my memory; it looks like the mess I left inside my room that I lost all courage to pick up one by one. It never stops reminding me that my days are disorganized, my world is a constant riot and my plans are still too blurry and uncertain.

Sometimes, my vacancy is like a casket filled with lies and judgments said by a lot of people who only met me on the surface, yet I was too towered by them that I allowed them to consume me, sometimes, they all look like the grave itself and the dead flowers that fell with it. The end of everything I wish to begin with again.

Sometimes, I am enraged like an ocean; too mysterious and too deep that people grew terrified that maybe I am the reason for their drowning without knowing that I, myself, am afraid of my own surging waves, afraid of my own depth, afraid of my own inconsistency.

I am tired of this life. I wish I could just end it. I wish I could live again without this. I wish I could sleep forever without having to worry about what my tomorrow will bring.

INDEFINITE DESPAIR

I still had some remnants of despair that I carried throughout this year. It was actually the time of my life where everything was disarranged and nothing seemed to fall into my favor. It was like the world was against me and I was so weak to fight alone. I was too feeble and too pointless. All my desires were out of my league, and none of them looked like they were within my reach. It was one of my down moments. The time of my life where my anxieties worsened, and I lost myself every single day. I barely recognized victories. I ran out of reasons to see the sunshine with hope and like it was completely inappropriate to force myself to be happy when I am not. There were days where everything around me seemed murkier than my dusks. It felt like I was never getting the opportunities that I was working hard for so long. I lost faith in myself and I lost the confidence that I once built so high before. Nothing seemed glowing and all sunsets were overtaken by my dawns.

It was so despairing yet I knew it'll keep happening. I thought there was no escape; I thought there was no exit door to this pain. My world was too messy that I could no longer bump on a brighter side. I thought it would last until I will give up and just leave everything behind and pain will numb me and will take over my entire system. I knew I was hard to love and it will be a risk falling for someone who doesn't know how to love herself.

So I stopped waiting for the world to stop my pain. I just keep waiting for my days to stop. Somehow, I learned to memorize the sadness.

I learned to name all of my despairs after all the bad memories as if they'll stay with me until the end of time.

HOW TO SAVE MYSELF

How am I going to save myself from my storms?
For I feel like a dead flower with many thorns.
When will learn to walk out from that door?
Or learn to paddle harder until I reach the shore?

How am I going to save myself from monsters?
When will I learn to find my way out from my pointless wanders?
It's like I keep writing the wrong plots, I'm the worst author.
And every time I fail, I feel growing smaller?

This grief started to invade my entire body.
It's like the world hated me as well as everybody.
I keep writing my fate on the page that's why I am a wrong story.
Maybe sulking on my own void became my hobby.

How am I going to save myself from all of these loud echoes?
It's like I drained myself from all the colors of yellow.

I was left with grey and blacks from my down below.

I was swallowed by grief until I lost my entire glow.

How am I going to save myself from all of these glares?

It's like being a room with no reserved chair.

Maybe I'll find my fixes on loneliness and beers.

And accept the reality that nobody wants to be my peer.

This grief started to invade my entire being.

I don't know where these waking moments are leading.

I want to spend the rest of my life dreaming.

But there I was, hoping someone would hear why I am screaming.

TELL ME

Tell me I am going to be better. Tell me I will be able to heal. Tell me there's a way out from this reverberating despair. Tell me I will get to see positivity again. Tell me there are unlimited chances and that there's always room to grow.

Tell me I needed to breathe once in a while. I needed to sound like I am certain of the things I haven't done yet. Tell me the world will one day start to listen and my heart will start to feel joy once again. Tell me there are hundreds of reasons to strive and that this despair will once day melt away from my system.

Tell me there are places I should venture out and my spirit will be restored again. Tell me I will be able to forgive, and I am able to forget these names and blood they gave to me. Tell me I will no longer sleep at night listening to my tears as if it's my lullaby. Tell me I am allowed to yell, and that the world will not hate me for being honest.

Someone, please tell me this is not yet the end, that there's something to look forward to. Tell me it is just a phase and I need to survive my worst storm. Someone, please tell me that this despair is just the start of everything I have to deal with and that it's here to teach me how to be strong. I needed someone to tell me this because I lost all energy to tell this to myself.

LEAVING SOON

I sat on my study table; thoughts were nibbling my bones. My questions were peeking. My answers were hiding. Somehow, I knew my days are counted. The ticking of the clock sounded more obvious than it was yesterday. My walls are slowly collapsing, and giving me a sight to places I abandoned for so long that I will abandon again soon. My sadness was so shrill I could feel it against my wrist. Everything around me will stay. Everything around me will remain how it used to. It will keep going soon but they will still remain.

Somehow, it's frightening to see all of them stay while I was there, never knowing what exact day or time I will leave and never come back again. All I knew was that —it'll be soon.

Nobody knew what it would be like to wake up each day and realize it's another day gifted to you. Sadly, it also gives you the trouble of thinking about tomorrow.

You didn't know if the day granted to you

to live is given just for you to live once again

or another day is given to you to say goodbye.

RUNNING AWAY

As the rain fell, my heart suddenly went a little hefty. All I heard were tiptoeing sounds of drizzle, slowly but surely turning into heavy rain. I lay down on my bed didn't know what to do. Everything around me taught me what loneliness was. My heart still breaks; my hopes were held high. My bedsheet untucked, my chest still stuffed with broken promises. My words were left unfinished from the poem I wrote on yellowish paper. Poems I left laid open at the top of my desk, the study light still on while the stars outside lost its glimmer. The screeching of tires from cars breaking the hush of another sad night.

Everyone's away. Everyone's unattended. Everyone's out of my sight. Everyone has forgotten me. I blended into the darkness. I blended with the silence. I made friends with my demons, for I thought they understood me the most. I caged my passion and left everything unfinished. I hated who I was. I hated who I am. I can't see who I will be.

Everything around me turns out to be like me as well —lost, torn, and broke. Everyone's tired. Everyone's unfilled.

Everyone's heading home only to find empty lifeless hallways.

I am running away from almost everything

because the world ran away from me as well.

WHAT WINTER TAUGHT ME

It was December.

My life used to run in such known errands, roads I have come to memorize because I've been there every day. I started missing the sun. I started missing the warmth of the day. Everything seemed to be more thriving when it's summer, but when the winter comes, all dreams turn dead, all excitements simmer, all worries deepened. They said winter is the saddest time of the year. Everything was almost grey, people were almost isolated, the sun has been rarely seen, and sadness remains the same.

I've always known who to evade and who to share a cup of coffee with; I always wanted to be the first to leave. I have always sorted my life in such ways that I learned how to stay out from circles that I wasn't certain to last long. I always wanted assurances, the things I knew I have to break no bones with.

I spoke words so cold and sharp like I was creating distance until I'm unreachable.

I built up bridges, and only those who have the nerve could burn them.

This is how life taught me; I need to stay away from those who will hurt me. I learned that the winter will soon fade, and their memories of me will soon be replaced.

IN WHATEVER LIFETIME

I love you, and I am slowly yet surely getting along with the reality that you're no longer here with us: to sleep next to me, to listen to my stories, to hear you laugh like there's no tomorrow. I knew losing you came with a contract of facing my present days longing for the past.

I am slowly accepting the truth that you're no longer here to wait for me to come home, to make me a cup of coffee, to tell me you miss me, to see that morning smile of yours first thing in the morning, to have someone I could watch movies together. I am slowly getting by, but I wanted to be stronger because I knew that's the only wish that you have before leaving me.

I love you. I wish I could rewrite us so I could change the things that made us fall apart. I wish I could tell you how much I want you back. I miss you so much it keeps hurting me, but I know you wanted me to get along with life. The pain still lingers, but you will always be the only person I will love forever.

You will always be the one I will love over and over again in whatever lifetime we will get the chance to meet again.

UNWANTED MEMORIES

How do we deal with the pain that never ceases to ache every time a single memory pays a visit? Is there anything we could do to blunt the sting or we just sat there on the floor, feel everything —savor every throbbing pain until we get used to it and that it'll numb me enough?

Sometimes, memories hold my softest parts. One minute I am fine then it only takes one memory to switch my mood into a storm I could not tame. It only takes a memory to make me dysfunctional and that I'll start hating myself for not being able to overcome the brokenness that made me look like scattered pieces of broken glass. The pain made me weaker while others, it made them stronger. I wonder when I will stop over feeling this pain because it grew a distance between understanding and hating myself. I want to know why I can't simply forget the pain that stays when the person who gave us the reason left already?

Are we able to deal with it by forgiving and make friends with the past? But are we able to forgive something that we don't truly understand?

It was just too hefty and too dense that it kills light every night, and I allowed darkness to take over my entire system. Maybe I grew so used to pain itself that I ended up welcoming it with open arms instead of threatening me to stop bothering me. It was ironic —just like what unwanted memories did to me.

CONTINUING LIFE

Life is not just about sunshine constantly greeting you outside your window first thing in the morning. It's not always about summer the whole year and expects that there'll be no rain. And I know you're living proof of how it feels dealing with constant rains while having no sight of hope. You've been through your worst storms, and you will always have great stories to tell about the mess it left on your floor.

The world has been filled up with so many negativities and closing doors. That everything was just too distant towards acceptance and toward understanding the depths. I know you deserve life the way you wanted it. You deserve a happy conversation with your friends as you tell them the name of someone who owns your heart. You deserve someone holding your hand without getting paranoid about who the people around are to see you, you deserve the light heart to show the world who you chose to love and break no single bone the moment you do it. I want the best for you. I know you deserve better.

But I also know you have your own good stories to tell about the soothing calm after it. You know the difference and that solitude after the storm had passed, and that's what survival is.

I am glad you've made it still.

WHAT WE ALL DESERVE

You deserve to breathe freely in front of everyone, with head up high and pride. You deserve the best of sunshine every Monday morning and warm greetings from a stranger who already seemed familiar to you. You deserve to have your heartbeat about the little things that come in the scope of your vision. You deserve to walk in the crowd without having people putting restriction lanes. You deserve the calmness of the sea, the way the sunset kisses its horizon. You deserve someone who will look at you with amazement and keep that moment in Polaroid so everyone else could see it. You deserve the summers inside your room as you sat at the edge of your bed, contemplating what kind of life you want. You deserve having it, every break, and starts. You deserve to choose the one who's right for you and will make you feel that you are close to perfection. You deserve everything. You deserve to receive the same love that your heart was keeping way too long ago.

I know you still have more stains and stings but I know that you are adept and strong to slowly unwelcome them out from you. Just take every minute that you needed for mending. No need for you to rush. Just take your time brave soul. Take all the time that you need. You're almost there. You're almost healing.

YOURSELF

You spend enough time holding that guilt inside your beating heart. You thought you were too much that everything you gave wasn't accepted. You became too much while you were becoming less for yourself. You slowly dim your own lights as you glimmer theirs. It gets a little frustrating and highly devastating. You ended up breaking your own bones for people who wouldn't even pick up a phone, for people who did nothing but hurt you without thinking about how vulnerable you are. You grew more for people who love to see you hurt yourself so you could aid them. And it's unfair. You were so used and abused and were asked for too much. You were so generous until it left you with nothing. You failed to look that you were becoming null and blank and just a black hole of overused wishes.

Somehow, you will acknowledge these lapses and will slowly draw yourself closer. You will start to draw the lines and step out from pages that don't involve you. You will grow from their negligence and you will learn to stand on your own you will thank yourself for taking the risk of starting again with yourself.

You grew yourself enough for them yet it never made them stay.

You need to learn how to be there for yourself sometimes.

TIME IS RIGHT

There'll be times when you'll start thinking that maybe the problem is you. The problem is your sadness. The problem is your addiction towards clinging into this darkness, to this silence, to this loneliness.

But then, you weren't sure if there's a way out if there's an exit door if there's anything that could help me escape from this prison mind. I don't know if there's a light at the end of the tunnel or I could build something out from ashes. You simply don't know. Nothing was certain. Nothing.

But then, every heartache has an attached lesson for you. Every pain holds the door towards taking chances and leaving those who stopped being good to you. Sometimes, you need to face endings so you could start once again. You need to start giving yourself the chances you gave to people who only breaks you.

It's okay to be selfish sometimes if that would mean saving yourself. It's okay to soar away from a crowd of people who only takes everything they are capable of taking. The world will still spin. The sun will still show up. The birds will still sings, the waves will still crash.

Everything will be okay.

It might not be now, but soon it will.

RELIVE

Little by little I wanted to pretend that I am not dying. I wanted to pretend that I am still in the midst of living my life. Somehow, I wanted to fill my time with new adventures. I wanted to make up for all of the lost adventures that I postpone for I thought I still have all the time that I needed. I wanted to see where my feet are escorting me, which mountain I could still climb on, where shores I could bury my feet with.

I wanted to reopen life like another present I received when I was a kid —excited, happy, and thankful. I guess it was just the thing I wished to be heard. I wanted to go back to the time where my happiness meant having all the little things. It was shallow, but I was satisfied. Now, wishing for days to extend and praying that my nights will not be my last night on earth gave me so many things to realize.

Now, as my days are shortened, everything started to compress into one single hope. I am not ready to live the life I have and face death when I still don't want to.

I wish the latest gift I would receive is an hourglass

where I could flip it back and start again when my time is up.

WONDERING

As I stare at my ceiling, I wonder what the stars look like on the other side of it. I wonder if the rain will soon arrive. I wonder about how my death would look like. Would it be in pain or in peace? I wonder if I will feel the physical anguish, or I would just sleep and never wake up again. I wonder about how they will see my dead, lifeless paled-skinned, and permanently gone body. I wonder how many people will see me, how many people will cry. I wonder how many people will remember me and will say they wished they stood beside me when they still had the opportunity.

I wonder who will be there on my wake, who will stare at my face and say I look pretty and at amity. I wonder how much I'll get to receive I-miss-yous. I wonder how many people will thank me for changing their lives, for making them feel at ease and remembered. I will wonder what memories they will recall when they say the eulogy.

I wonder about who will be there when I die.

I wanted to know if just like me,

they regretted the time they lost

because they thought we have forever to live.

GOES ON

This sadness is addicting and dragging. It's been swallowing you out alive. All you were left of were glooms inside the drawers of your table, rains inside your bedroom, and spilled ink of your tears you will never run dry with. All you have were empty canvass of encouragement from people who stopped lifting you up and a comical grudge towards yourself.

Maybe you were just used to feeling this, how belongingness meant light-years away. You were so used to the idea that everyone has their own errands to run with and everyone stopped paying attention to your emotional needs. You can't blame. You know you can't. You began putting distance because everything you touch, you ruin. Everything that's ruined became too incapable to return from perfect pieces. You believed you were a walking disappointment, horrendous destruction, and maybe just too much for people. But you wanted someone to be there.

I hope time will soon help you heal all the wounds you never grew tired of scratching from time to time. I hope you will be able to understand the meaning of redirection. Somehow, you have to believe yourself enable to see what's on the other side chances.

Life goes on, and all you need to do is to get by.

LETTERS OF ABUSE

It was a fine afternoon; I sat alone on a bus next to a woman whose face was covered by a thick scarf. She wore long sleeves in hot weather. I can barely see her face clearly, but she seemed uneasy. She stood up on the first stop. I noticed she left a worn notebook, but it was too late to catch her since the bus has already started. I know it was bad to read something that wasn't yours, but I found myself sinking on the first painful page. She wrote:

"When you lost the person who you used to be, you began spending so many nights wondering where it went and if there's a chance for it to come back. I knew I changed a lot.

I changed so much that I could no longer recognize how I used to define the exact shade of happiness that I used to have. I used to be good at everything. I used to be very dedicated to the things I was interested in and that I also knew that I was indeed running after to the difficult one until I learned how to understand the complexities. I always knew my priorities—I used to have that standard where I tend to organize my priorities.

Everyone gets to meet someone who will change everything in just one snap and that sometimes, everything started to look like pretty fictions that were so enticing and triggered you to leave your own reality. He was my game-changer. He was the plot twist that came out in the middle of nowhere. Over that course, he gave me reasons to stare at when I was blinded by my own frustrations. He was the person who embraced the scars I inflicted on my skin. He was enough. He made me feel that I was more than enough. We were enough. My love for him overpowered me. It also gave him the power to use it against me.

I thought he'll remain as my safe zone, my constant. But then I saw myself slowly losing myself while loving him. He sometimes loves me. He sometimes hurt me —physically, emotionally mentally. And I don't know which *hurts more, knowing he won't change or knowing I can't change who my heart wants after all."*

THE SECOND PAGE

I flipped on the second page. The words still stung:

"Another day, yet the same heartbreak.

In an instant, I didn't care about what I will lose, I didn't care about the things that I have to let go from my grip just so I could hold him. But slowly, I was also letting go of myself in the process. I was slowly drifting away until I could no longer recognize myself alone if I was not with him. I allowed him to take over my system until I didn't realize that my love for him held me hostage from seeing a wider work. I did it for him. I did it for love. I was empty for affection and belongingness that I permitted his strength to invade my veins.

He was the thing I learned to memorize, so I clung to him. I held on although sometimes, his hands gripped me so tightly that I had trouble breathing. Sometimes, they clasp with names dug on my skin I refused to label as abuse. I was afraid to change because of his changes.

The thing about loving so much is you thought it was something that really belonged to you. I was holding tight to what was temporary hoping I could make it permanent. I was taking every wrong road hoping the world will one day get tired of disappointing me.

What hurts me most was knowing that no matter what I do, he will never willingly stretch an arm to welcome me for an embrace. I carried all inside my chest, and the day after, they it got heftier and started taking control of me. Rejection took me as their favorite target, and I never knew what diverging meant. I allowed him to hurt me until my scars reminded me of my fragility.

One of the biggest frustrations I had was knowing that the person who was supposed to stitch me back together again became one of the reasons why I was falling helplessly apart.

He was supposed to help me protect myself from the cruelty of the world, but in my case, he showed to me that one of the scariest places to be was being with him."

STAYED

The third page hit differently. It's like being in her shoes and seeing the hell she's been through:

"I trusted myself and my decisions enough to stay with him. I was so assured that it's him that I could see myself growing old with, building a home with, sharing success, and the same hand I would hold while I am working hard to reach my goals. The same one I see myself marrying one day when the right time comes. He became this someone that taught my heart how to love unconditionally, with no pause or times-outs. I enjoyed loving him with all of me. I enjoyed giving everything even the ones that were supposed to belong to me. I wanted to prove to him that I loved him the same, that even after the times that he already had me and all the promises I kept reminding him that I will never leave him. I am still the woman he loved since day one and that I am getting better for us. He knew how

much I loved him. He knew how willing I was to lose myself if that would mean his gain.

But I guess, time changes people, and sadly, it changed him. I was too blinded towards my love for him that I never realized that he was only taking everything he was capable of taking. He slowly stopped giving love like how he used to. He took things for granted and took advantage of my love for him. I was okay because I loved him. I tried to be okay because I knew that not all relationships are perfect. I tried to understand him although most of the time, I was slowly getting tired trying to understand his nightmarish changes. He stopped being the man I loved for so long. Instead, he became the man I could no longer recognize who has only hurt me like my heart was nothing but another storage of forgiveness and endless patience. He grew violent as if my skin was nothing but a paper he could tear; my heart suddenly felt like another fragile thing that he was gradually adding patches of pain without even asking if I was capable to carry the ache.

He became a monster that I lost all right to tame. But I stayed. After all the abuse, I still chose to stay."

MY FRAGILITY

I told myself I should stop reading, but somehow, I was curious about what happened. I need to know if she's okay, so I continued to read the next page:

"I stayed wishing that I would one day wake up and that he would return to be the same man I used to love. I wanted to save us from constant break out, but every time I do so, I have to sacrifice my worth; I have to sacrifice a big part of me. I have to set aside myself, so I could lift him up although I knew I was leaving myself in the pool of anxieties to drown. I was hurting myself day and night just because I kept choosing him despite the pain he never stopped giving me. He suddenly replaced all my excitement toward building a future alongside him with bruises I tried my best to conceal behind clothes. He suddenly stopped giving me kisses instead he started serving me hurtful words that I was never prepared to hear. Sometimes, he said it at dinner, and I swallowed everything hoping that if let everything slide down;

I would receive peace in return. But I was so damn wrong. He took everything in me that he was able to break such as my fragility and my soft parts. He kept hurting me because he knew that I would stay despite it all. After all, that's how I wanted to prove to him that he would always be my true love. He started to look like the man I used to love, but he came up to me like a stranger who made love look violent and mad. I was afraid to the point that I wished I could just escape him —that I could find my way out from him."

FINALLY FREE

I was on the last page. The pain intensified and my heart got torn so bad.

"And when I finally did, I knew it was the last best thing that I could do for myself. I should've done that a long time ago instead of watching his monster take in control of my life and happiness. I knew not everyone understood why I had to leave him. Nobody saw what was happening within those years. They thought we were both happy and I was just uncontended. But what they didn't know was that the years I spent trying to save us from falling apart, the days I wish I cried myself to sleep hoping that tears could cleanse all the cuts he left in my skin. Nobody knew about the pain that I had to digest just to prove to everyone that I was not only there to stay with him during good weather. I stayed with him on his storms, on his worst days until he turned mine into one. I have loved him so much that I tried my best to stay with him despite how tired I was.

I loved him, and he knew that. I loved him so much, and he used it to take me for granted. I loved him so much I emptied myself. And I know it's time to regain my worth, it's time to regain my loss. I needed to love my shattered self. I needed to let him go, so this time, I could hold on to myself. I always believed I could be more for him until I had enough.

So I am writing this and will plan to escape. I'll ride a bus and allow my feet to take me to wherever it might be. I will bring with me the freedom that I deserve. I am writing this, so I can take this ugly past away from my memory. I'll transfer this to these sheets and will drop this when I have to.

So to you, reading this. I hope you'll never allow love to empty you. Love when you feel like you want to. Leave if you feel like you need to."

THE WINTER IN HER

She always told him she's a winter. He never believed her. She said it only takes his warmth. She believed, but she was afraid. Perhaps, it was because she knew herself enough than he knew. She knew what her winter would look like. It would obscure his sun; it would eradicate all remnants of summer. It would make the world turn gloomy, less adventurous, and deserted.

She always told him she's a winter. He almost believed her. She said that she'll melt away all her struggles and bring her back to liveliness. She believed him. She always found herself wanting to believe him because he sounded sincere, he sounded real. She set aside her indifference and got lost in his promises.

She always told him she's a winter. He stopped believing her and decided to desert her. He realized he couldn't handle her winter well, so he walked out and started searching for someone who will complement his summers. She was deeply hurt. Her heart turned cold. She killed every possibility of happiness and froze her heart next to anger.

She was so cold and remained aloof. She despised her triggers, she despised her wintriness words and affections. She wanted his summers —at least for once.

And she can't hate him, so she hated herself instead.

COLD HEART

The winter has arrived; the first snow fell. Everyone's waiting for this time to come. All thick coats were used, all bonfires were lit. The chimneys reminded me of the carols and Christmas songs. The kids were running back and forth, throwing snowballs to anyone they could. Smiling faces reassembled; completeness is foreseen. Everyone found their way home.

These sights were always anticipated and seen clearly from my window. I would have sat there, half of my body hiding behind a thick blackout curtain. Everyone got a hand to hold, everyone had someone they could call for at the end of the day to share the good thing. The snowman would soon be built and the bonfires would soon be lit.

I sat there thinking about life. Everyone's so excited about the cold weather while I was there realizing that I had it all my life. Coldness through the responses that I received from my loved ones. Coldness from the hand who no longer loved me.

Coldness in words I could no longer cage out. Coldness from the past I never got over it. Coldness from the dreams I turned my back from.

It's pretty wintry; my heart has always been this cold even without it.

UNFORGOTTEN WINTER

That year, she remembered the first day of winter. She wore her nicest clothes, put on her expensive and rarely used makeup, and dressed like it's her last day. She was a little terrified, but she waited for this day to happen. She was about to tell him that she liked her. Chances were slim but she wanted to believe that there are miracles in winters. Folks say that confessing your feelings to someone on the first snow will make everything possible.

As she stood in front of him, her hands were numb; her heart was beating too fast and too loud. She's about to say the words she practiced for years. As she told him that she liked him, his smile turned into confusion. He said nothing that nothing was something she understood: unreciprocated, unreturned, blameless. She had no choice but to understand and accept his choice.

The first snow became her witness. She stopped believing in the miracle of winters. It was her first heartbreak that still twinged her heart when snow started falling on the first day.

That confession haunted her.

His silence remained loud and still breaks her.

It froze her fate and hated love after then.

IT WAS WINTER

Winter was a bit different —it's like everything that I wanted to forget suddenly knocked on my door. It was winter when I lost you. It was winter when you finally decided to leave me after so many years of trying. It was winter that you made up your mind.

The sight of you leaving with your bag filled with final decisions remained in my memory. I still see it even if I close my eyes. I still see it every time I fall to sleep. The winter reminded me of the time that I lost everything. It reminded me about how you never returned.

That's why I can't stand the idea of winter. It's more than just loneliness. It's more than just sadness. It's me wishing you will one day return. It's me wishing you will find your way back to me. It's me hoping it's not yet too late to forgive, so we could forget and start all over again.

But winter has come. Winter has gone. Nothing happened. You still didn't make it.

But I am still wishing that when the world has turned its back on you, you will find your way back to me.

I am hoping it'll be a little different again.

It was winter when I lost you. I hope winter would bring you back to me as well.

HOW ABOUT TOMORROW?

The silence was deafening. The atmosphere was too eerie, and staring at the white casket gave me the slap of reality that nothing will be the same again.

They always say that it's okay to deal with someone who walks away and decides to live in a faraway place. That longing is completely bearable because at one point, it gives you a small optimism that your paths will cross again; however, losing someone and knowing that they are no longer a part of this world give us so much pain that crying until you run out of tears will never be enough. The pain of knowing that you will never see that person forever leaves a hole in our chest that will forever haunt us with million faces of what-ifs.

As I sat here staring at that white casket in front of me, my thoughts became too dark that made me wish I could just turn back the time. I wish that there's more that I could do. The person lying inside that coffin was the most important person in my life; it'll take forever to let go of this ache.

I wish I could see that person the next day and that nothing about death has ever happened. It's completely hard to sabotage the pain because it lives inside my head.

It's hard saying I miss you to the person

who's now a dead body and knowing I could no   longer see him tomorrow.

DISBELIEF

People were wondering what happened; it was why all of a sudden, and why him out of all the million people in the world. They kept asking questions as if we knew the answer. None of us was prepared, and that funeral night was filled with queries that flashback the pain that never seemed to subside.

I went in front of your coffin and you looked like you were just sleeping peacefully with no pain and no worries on your young face. You look like you were just taking a slumber from this noisy world, and maybe that's why I was having a hard time understanding why I should stop waiting for you to wake up. I knew you were gone permanently and that spending the next day without you was just too much to bear; that's why I wanted to avoid everyone asking why you were gone. I can't swallow the truth that I have to go on with living when the person who gave me the best motivations to keep going would no longer join me to face the odds of the world.

Being at your funeral was the greatest torture. It was like every second was filled with reminders that there's no way I could replace reality with my daydreams.

It was like I had no choice but to slap my face over and over again

Just so I wake up and accept that I lost you.

I can't believe I lost you and that was it.

LONGING

Your last night here was the most miserable night that I had to endure. The echoes of people's sympathetic murmurs were bouncing on the four walls of the funeral home. All these yellow lights were blinding me. I wanted to cry as much as I could; I had given so much since the first day that I was left with nothing but emptiness to deal with.

They kept asking me if I was fine. Of course, I was never fine. I would never be fine. I didn't know how to be fine but somehow, I had no choice but to tell myself that I was okay because I didn't want to leave a burden in their memory as soon as they leave. They started narrating the stories they had with you; all the memories they made with you. I sat there holding back myself from bursting because they saw the goodness in you. I always knew you were the best person out there and that they appreciate your existence. My body was about to collapse, for I couldn't bear to listen to experiences they had with you because the pain of missing you stopped me from seeing even just a spark of happiness.

I knew everybody loved you because you left a mark on their lives just like what you did to mine. You left a never-fading memory that would make all of us smile when we bump on something that will remind us of you someday.

That night —that last night of your funeral

was just the beginning of my everyday battle of missing you.

HOW ABOUT TOMORROW?

It's time for the burial. Everyone wore white while I wore a visible pain. I saw the sky covered with gray clouds as if even the heaven above was about to cry with us. The prayer was spoken and heard, and then it hit me; I would no longer see your face.

I stared blankly at your casket, and it was as if I was silently talking to you. I whispered that I wished you'll never forget me; that in the next life, we would get to see each other again; and that we would recognize the love that we had on the next time we meet. I sat there for half an hour, I recalled all the best memories that we had; you never failed to love me without conditions. I saw a black butterfly land on your flower standee. I assumed it was you saying goodbye to us. I assumed it was you telling us that you're okay with your fate and that we should face tomorrow with acceptance.

I stared too long that I never knew my cheeks were flooded with so many tears. It came cascading, and my chest tightened. It was by then that I realized that emotional pain could be too much it started to ache physically.

I hope you'll find your way to visit us through our dreams because we are not ready to let go yet.

Not now.

Not yet.

CRUEL WORLD

That was it —the last day, the last stare on your sleeping face, and the last sight I could have in your physical body before the ground slowly eats your flesh away from your bones. That was it, the last time I could ever get close to you physically. I started crying, and my tears fell on the glass of your coffin like raindrops too heavy that I could no longer hold it back.

I cried so hard, I asked the Man above to listen to my prayers. I was asking Him to wake me up from this nightmare because I couldn't believe that I wouldn't see you again. I started crying and pleading to bring you back to us because our life would never be complete again. I cried horribly to the point that I lost my composure. Everyone around me knew the pain I was suffering as it was written all over my face. They pulled me back to the chair while I was resisting. I couldn't let the earth take you away from us. I couldn't. I just couldn't.

I guess I was too powerless and too ordinary that I had no choice but to allow the world to run my fate no matter how unfair it was. It started raining hard; I watched your casket slowly being lowered down on the graveyard.

The world was crying along with me.

The world knew how much I hate goodbyes.

The world knew it so damn well,

yet the world took you away from me.

MAYBE

"I sometimes wonder how you made it," she said; her tears were almost as weighty as her words. "I wonder how you managed to keep her like your dirty secret, how she became the woman behind your secret smiles, and how you conquered the guilt of lying to me just to be with her. I wonder how you stopped thinking about the damage it will give me. I thought my pain was also your pain? I thought you held on to that promise that you will be the only person who will save me from this unswerving pain that life gives? I thought it was you who will make me feel that I am enough and that you will not find my shortages to someone else? That's why I don't understand why there has to be her and you when it was supposed to be me and you. Just us. Just the two of us. I don't understand why there have to be lies and secrets when I used to be the only person you shareD the things you never shared with anyone else. You trusted me and made me the closet of your foolish skeletons. Now, you made her as one yet you never allowed her bones to slip from your own closet — a closet that I didn't know existed.

Maybe she was pretty something. Maybe she made you feel things. Maybe she's quite different from me. That's why you allowed yourself to be tempted? Maybe I was missing something. Maybe, I turned out to be just your another "maybe."

INFIDELITY

"I imagine her being there with you," she started writing these words on a blank sheet of paper. Her hands were shaking from the collision of anger and pain. Her room felt like it's winter inside and her heart stopped beating for a little while.

"It hurts," she continued writing. It pains me to think that there was another character in our plot that I was completely unaware of. I don't know which would hurt more: knowing she had you secretly or knowing that you allowed her to take you away from me. I wanted to blame her. I wanted to hate her until my words could kill her, but then I realized, maybe you weren't that faithful enough that you ended up saying yes to her. I wanted to blame her, but maybe she wouldn't have pursued you if you had closed your door before she even knocked.

I don't know where I should pour this heavy pain that I feel because you two are the reason for this. I was just in love and I was just being loyal because that's what a relationship should be. That's why, I don't understand why you had the decency to be with her and me —both at the same weight and time. I don't understand why it has to hurt the person who did nothing but just love with all honesty.

I want to blame you. I want to blame her. I want to blame temptation for existing, yet here I am, blaming myself for allowing this fate to happen.

THE HEART NEVER FORGETS

"It was me," he said.

The words hit like a tidal wave the moment she heard it.

"It was me and my stupidity. It was me and my imprudence. It was all my fault because I allowed her to ruin us. I allowed that few months to break down the years that we spent together into hopeless tatters that I could no longer put back to its perfect shape. The cracks will remain and I know I will spend the rest of my life asking you to forgive me. I know you will forgive but I know you enough that your heart never forgets not even a minute of it. I know the pain will keep coming back to wake you up in the middle of the night. I know the pain will give you reasons to doubt love and to trust the process once again. This is the damage that it will give you and I can't blame you if you stop choosing us.

She was something new to me and perhaps I got intrigued. I was tempted by the idea of trying new things again. It's like going on an adventure. I thought I could stop it. I thought one mistake was enough, but I was so damn wrong. It went on and on. I permitted temptation to cloud my sanity away.

I am so sorry, for I ended up owing you an apology when I promised I was not going to hurt you. I am sorry because I stopped being the man I promised you I would be. I am sorry for I was tempted.

I am sorry because I know you didn't deserve this.

Not at all."

THE TRUTH KNOWS HOW TO KNOCK

Temptation happens when one person starts indulging in doing something wrong. She must have been your "something wrong". She must have been that meantime pleasure that you thought you could eradicate in the picture anytime you want as if nothing happened. You thought you could spend the rest of your life burying the secret alive and never leaving traces. You thought you could let that temptation remain as an unheard story forever. You thought you could keep the truth away from me and look at me straight in the eyes as if nothing happened behind my back, but you were wrong. I always knew you better than myself that's why I knew that something was going on behind my back. It took me a long time to read between the hints but I knew something was definitely wrong. When I found out about your affair, about your infidelity, I realized I was just too mystified to the point that I thought I was just trapped in a nightmare and soon, I will wake up. Soon, you'll be back to tell me my mind was just playing tricks on me.

That day never came. I didn't wake up from that nightmare because they became my reality. They became the real death of me. I was so flabbergasted every time I get to uncover one truth. I still don't know how I am going to put myself back into whole again. It keeps recalling. It keeps replaying. It keeps hurting.

UNFORGIVEN

I want to say that I am sorry. I know it may arrive insufficient since the damage has already been done, but for now, it feels like I need to let you know how I regret everything that I did to hurt you, how I permitted the fleeting temptation to break us apart. I want to let you know that I am very guilty. I must be honest; I was never really happy upon hurting you. I know that there's nothing I could do to ease the pain I gave you. Everything appears so small that my sincere words of apologies won't stitch a broken wound. It was too much that I could not repair it with my suitcase of sorries and regrets. I am the most stupid person for cheating on you. I love you. It might sound ironic to hear that, but I really do. I realized how much I love you when you're now on verge of walking away. I wasn't sure about how I ended up in that place and started entertaining someone other than you. I know we had promises that we should live up to despite the distance between us; however everything happened in fast forward, and I was just right there, deviating myself from the heartache you gave me by insisting that I should enjoy somebody else' company.

Regardless of how blurry the sequences were, all I could ever remember was that I was desperate to swerve what was killing me and that was loving you. I was left with no choice and power to pull you close beside me. I was hurting, and I was so frantic to save myself from how I made it a daily routine of serving myself with poison for loving someone who was once sure of me. I am sorry for breaking your trust. I am sorry because I am no longer the person you thought I would be.

"Winter always comes to an end, always."
—Maxime Lagace

Endless Spring

"The beautiful spring came, and
when nature resumes her loveliness,
the human soul is apt to revive also."
—Harriet Ann Jacobs

WHAT MADE YOU BRAVE

I slept tired, and I wake up still tired.
I wonder how many times I tried.
So many flowers bloomed and died.
So many drowning I had been against my own tides.

I sometimes hate the sight of my own defeat.
I knew the more I insist the more I became incomplete.
I don't know where I am taken by these feet.
Somehow, I grew so used to how life was indeed bittersweet.

I get a little lost sometimes.
There were moments my poems no longer rhyme.
And how I ended up losing my words in between the lines.
There were days I depend on my fate on signs.

I didn't know how long I can make it.
But despite how hard it was, I don't want to quit.
I'd still want to try until I find a place I truly fit.

I need to face it all up with courage and wit.

Somehow I learned what bravery means.
No matter how ugly the world might be in between.
You just need to emerge clean.
You keep trying even if daylight was not yet seen.

It's okay to be lost for days or weeks.
To be able to survive something that's unbelievably bleak.
Being able to accept and conquer loneliness and to others. You don't speak.
To be brave means its okay to be weak.

GROWING UP FAST

Every time I see children running wild and free on the rusty playground, the image of my young self eventually flashes back. These children running on uneven grounds without the fear of stumbling down. Their daughter was so loud; the word embarrassment was unsuitable for their innocence. Both boys and girls living to the fullest while they still have time. These children knew that happiness only requires small things. Happiness is free and attainable.

We think happiness is about those fleeting moments of getting what you want. We thought that when we grew up, we could take everything we wanted. Permanent happiness is actually much more complex, but much more worthwhile. They all have it now —the children. They clearly have it now but they're still too young to understand. Still too young to appreciate.

Somehow, when they'll start to grow old and they are no longer children, they will look back to their childhood like what I do now. They will reminisce how time moved so fast and then they're no longer allowed to do these things that they used to.

They will miss it, like how I miss it now.

SHE WONDERS

This is to all the children who are secluded, who felt like they belonged to loneliness. This is to all the children who lost all their courage, for those who see the sadness on rainy days. This to children who have no choice but to work hard when they should have been there, playing and learning. This is to all the children who feel like they're too tired at their young age, too weak to do things they weren't supposed to. This is for them who hope for better days, who hoped for the storms to pass, for the calmness to follow after.

This is for them who wished nothing but to breathe without having to worry about the pressures and exhaustion that tomorrow might bring. This is for them who wished for peaceful nights, for precisions, for being another priority. This is to all of the children who wished they have a home to go to, have a comfortable bed to sleep on, and loving parents who will unleash their plights out from their systems.

I hope you all find peace, I hope that as you all look back to this phase, you will find yourself smiling and call it a good experience. This is to all the children who were torn down, used, and abused. May your heart be filled with courage.

May you find happiness after the long audible sadness.

I hope it's not yet too late to start something new again.

THE HOPE THAT FORM IN THIS FRIENDSHIP

Our friendship was one of those things that stayed with me for the longest time. It gave me hope when I was so enveloped with so many negativities. It exceeded so many terms and surpassed so many records from people who gave me temporary promises. Our friendship was the one that stood with me through the test of time, and you gave me such amazing journeys, the ones that I kept inside my heart and restore them on my memory. Our friendship was never the perfect one, but we had the best things to remember. You gave me shelter when I was visited by my storms. I gave you the calm when you just wanted the storm to pass by.

We have been there together, stitching each other's wounds with presence, replacing fictions into realities. We have been there telling each other how it feels to be in love for the first time, how we watched each other's heartbreak because we believed the lies that we were enticed to accept.

We were there telling the moon to admire its craters and never get intimidated by how the stars shone. We were there for us, building our friendship by bricks made of trust and love, of years and memories worth retelling. We were each other's support systems, where every code was memorized, every silence was expected, and every unsaid word was understood. Everything that was never written in the line was tangible to the two of us.

Without you, I might have been spending my days constantly getting lost.

You gave me love and hope.

MEETING YOU

As I hold your hand, I knew we met for a reason.
The warmth gave me a shred of a summer season.
It's like the sun slowly sulking to embrace the horizon.
As your words filled with wisdom always give me lessons.

The thought of you helps me know how to restart
From the days where I almost grew apart.
How I found the hope that came crashing like a dart.
When it comes to love, you taught me how to be life-smart.

I was never someone's first, not second nor third,
And times where hope appeared blurred.
There were so many lies that I already heard.
And many promises that were just too slurred.

Loving you made all roads straight.
And every buckle suddenly lost all its weight.

I know both of us a wonderful tale that our histories made.

And everything will be aligned, it will be our fate.

All of a sudden, all wounds were fixed by a kiss.

Hope froze the pain that already exists.

The many mistakes that I can't untangle, I can't untwist.

And healing knocked on my door because right love persists.

The thought of meeting you because of fate became my escape,

How you wanted to be in my life, and take seats that you wanted to partake.

I know I am not perfect, and I have my crucial mistakes.

But you love me right, and my heart was finally free from hate.

IS THERE LESSON IN LIFE?

I wonder what my struggles are trying to teach me. I wonder why this pain has to be this shrill, why my self-worth has to be so blurry to the point that I ended up hating myself for becoming something that I am not. I wonder what this life is teaching me. Do I really have to go through a difficult path for me to understand that everyone has to go through one? Do I really have to plant hatred in my heart for me to feel that my heart is alive?

Does life really have to teach me the lessons by tearing me apart first? By putting emphasis on the things that I am incapable of? Sometimes, I wonder how it was going to last long because I knew it already and these lessons that life's teaching me don't truly work out.

It only makes things worse, it only makes me feel discouraged. I wanted to isolate my entire self away from the world's threat of facing realities. I don't know how to keep the strings attached anymore. I just want everything to be done; I want

to see the sunlight. I want to see life the way others
see it.

*I know life is teaching me to be strong but
why I always ended up feeling sorry for myself.*

REMEDY

Burning —my hands are craving for the touch of a paintbrush, for a stroke, for colors, for an empty canvass. I am searching for an outlet to pour this throbbing, this confusion, this anger, this madness, this love, and excitements. I want to paint everything that I captured through my eyes and stored in my memory. I want to recall every edge of this world that I almost thought I would fly if I jump. I am thinking about all of these stories that I could convert to portraits.

It's my healing; it's my way of forgetting the world for turning out so cruel. It's my way of forgetting the people who forgot me. It's my way of listening to what my mind is telling me, it's my way of letting them out one by one until I am able to start anew. Through feeding my passion with love and desire, I can breathe once more, I am able to see life from a different angle, in a good background —in ways that I am free to modify.

Through this passion, I was able to keep moving, to find more colors to fill my sheets and change dull things into something magical.

My love and passion aided me. It redirected me. It helped me survived. It helped me lived.

NURTURED BY WISDOM

No matter where you go, no matter how dark the nights could be at some time, no matter how many times people shouted at you to keep your hush —never stop learning. Never stop running after keys to unlock wisdom. You need it. The world is a little loud, a little horrible, and unpleasant, and the only way to replace the ignorance is by using the wisdom that you accumulated through experience. Every weakness is capable of turning into power; silence will one day turn into a clinging voice. Everything will turn into colors as you feed it with your wisdom.

Never allow everyone to tell you to stop exploring. Never allow them to point to you where you should only go. Never allow them to stop you from sprinting to new places that hold a new point of view. Never allow them to limit what to read and what to write. Never allow them to stop your heart from thriving towards never learning. The knowledge that you need: Turn it into wisdom in no time. Make it easy for you to live life in terms that you understand. Make it easy for them to see that you're someone who's meant to rise and not just sloop down or being stepped on.

Just keep growing. Always take everything that nurtures your wisdom.

CALM AFTER THE STORM

After the rains comes rainbows.
The cold wind still blows.
Parked cars are still in a row.
The city has been cleansed to glow.

After painful nights comes new mornings.
Another chance to see a reason for learning.
You understood why the rain has been pouring.
Opportunities are still there —calling.

After silence comes a new thought to ponder.
The pain will soon reside; you will learn to conquer.
It will help you become a little stronger.
You'll find calmness in the sound of thunders.

After a long journey, the view has always been worthy.
The future is no longer your worry.
You will learn to adjust to the speed —no need to hurry.
Life is always filled with such splendid glory.

Somehow, there were moments when the world is a no better place.

As well as sincerity was unseen on other's face.

But somehow, I believed there's always grace.

Answers arrive when it has too for you to embrace.

When you feel like you've been left out by the rest.

When personal life has been filled with endless stress.

Always remember that you did your best.

At least you did, take that sadness off your chest.

THE TRAGIC FATE

For some reason, despite the way we looked almost the same, we felt an incompletion. We still needed approval—from the people who gave you life and unconditional love. We were accepted, but they left us a wrong card on the table that I took courageously because I had no choice. It was easy for me to say we could make it but it's truly hard when destiny wanted s apart. Words came out just to justify my love for you but I realized they came out like poisons served for me every single day. We stood together despite my hesitation. I watched you take the further steps, how you left your religion to lessen the complexities. I watched how difficult it is for you to leave the things you were used to, the faiths you upheld for so long since you were a kid. It was really difficult for you to go against the will of your parents as you gave up your faith because you were so unsure about it lately. I knew I broke their trust that was not established well yet, that you have to endure their sharp words for sacrificing your religion because you wanted to prove something for yourself. You wanted to test yourself and stand over something that was bothering you. You wanted to be on the good side and be mediocre. You proved something for yourself.

Maybe that's how it was. Some destinies must be accepted even if it means saying goodbye and knowing they'll never return.

WHAT FAME GAVE ME

Fame brought me too many places —places I have never been to. It brought me to many highs and lows, to many foreign and local lands. Fame took me to the best sites that have spectacular views, the one that speaks nature at the background of my photos. It brought me to the most peaceful cities, to the most cynical regions of the world where stars shone so bright, where the sun screams hate and summer and waves kissing my toes as I leave footprints on its sand.

Fame made me meet new people —people I only see before on screens; people I was so curious to know. I saw them. All of them standing in front of me. Their smiles were so wide and contagious. Most of my wonders were answered; some of them became my friend. I saw myself living in a life where I thought would only happen in my imaginations.

But behind all that, fame brought me too many criticisms. Fame brought me to the hate, to judgments, to torn privacy, to unsecured homes.

Fame gave me the creeps; the constricted life I never knew I'll end up missing. It brought me to something I never knew I was capable of.

Some days I was happy. Most days I was not. It turned me into someone that I was not.

STAY BRAVE

Life has always been filled with a series of uncertainties. Uncertainties in such a way that there were days when your happiness reached the peak of a mountain and on some nights, you found yourself slowly drowning from your own puddle of tears. There were days when your life was pure adventures, wandering the corners of the world with bravery and positivity, and on some days, you found yourself stranded in your room, never wanting to come out, never wanting to see the world. You found yourself slowly blending in the darkness and there you knew you are lost. There will be days when you could get what you need without trying your hardest to have it but lately, everything appeared like they're so far from your reach; even the dreams were loosen out from your grasp.

Sometimes, everything looked like it's was there to stay but sometimes, nothing seemed permanent and casually wobbling from your touch.

You found yourself slowly embracing the darkness and hoping that you will one day get used to it. Life is all about balance. It's all about feeling sad so you'll understand the importance of happiness. You need to know what pain is so you'll discover your fragility. You need to risk so you'll know what survival is.

Keep healing.

Keep trying.

Stay courageous.

FLOWERS IN SPRING

Hummingbirds always sing.
Colors are what flowers bring.
The field is filled with radiant things.
Nature has always been different when it's spring.

The clouds faded its gloom.
The flowers started to bloom.
Vases were placed inside the rooms.
Optimism glows and looms.

Flowers are seen everywhere.
On bouquets, they wanted to share.
Flowers breathe in the same air.
It blossoms from here and there.

The dead ones were replaced by new ones.
It has always been kissed by rains and sun.
It made the place look more fun.
On flower fields, I'd like to take a run.

Just like flowers, it'll be my turn someday.
My words will blossom on its way.

The radiance will make surely stay.
It'll make the place enticing for a play.

As the current goes from that calm river.
And the wind continues to whisper.
As much as you want to thrive forever,
The flowers someday soon unfortunately wither.

SIGHT OF FOREVER

When I was young, I pictured out what love would look like when I finally understood it. I would always take Mama and Papa as the epitome of forever. When I was a kid, Mama would merrily get up from bed to prepare breakfast. Papa would follow her in the kitchen, kiss her forehead, and tell her good morning with nothing but certainty, softness, and gentleness in his voice. Mama would ask Papa what he likes, and Papa would pick pancakes over a club sandwich.

They would tease each other, swap duties when one has to go to the bathroom for baths. Papa would make coffee for Mama and strawberry milk for me. They would spend an hour at the table as we take our breakfast. Papa would talk about his expectations and Mama would listen wholeheartedly. I barely understood the concept of forever back then, but I saw these simple sights of my parents, and I can't help but admire them. They never demand greater things. One talks while the other listens. One would lend a hand if needed.

So that was my morning sight ever since I was a kid. I would never get tired of playing it repeatedly inside my head.

Their love for each other taught me that forever is a long time, but spending it with the person you love makes everything possible.

WHAT MAKES YOU BEAUTIFUL

Stay kind, and your kindness will take you to places. May you continue to soar and never get your eyes off from the sight. May you continue chasing good days with determination and always remember to do good things to everyone you meet on your way. Always love the right people and leave the ones who put doubts in your capabilities. Always believe in yourself, before anyone else does. Bring your best in everything that you do. May you have the most precious and unforgettable day today. I wish you will paint such a memory of how many people really admire you and take you as our special someone. You will always be different, and that's why you're distinguishable.

You always stand out and you deserve every blessing and massive chance that comes and will come your way because the world witnessed your pureness. You are the sweetest and the rarest. So believe me when I say that your kindness will take you to places. It will take you to the tallest mountains for you deserve a spectacular view. It will take you to the best people who will treat you so much better. It will take you to so many opportunities until you can find that courage to pursue your passion.

Your kindness is what makes you more than beautiful.

REMEMBER LOVE THIS WAY

I know, love is a bit confusing and tends to give you more questions hanged above your head like clouds gathered enough evaporation and ready to pour any time of the day. I know it's more of an irony when it was supposed to be a question. It brings more blank spaces, and you have to take and wait for much secured time just to fill them with the ink of a great tale of why love is worth a jump and a try.

I wanted you to believe in love and only remember the happiness you got from it. I hope it will weigh more than the sadness and disappointments of how love never stayed for you before.

And I am here. I am here to tell you that love is a place you could run to when the world is too clamorous. I wanted you to run for me and see that love is solace and that you're allowed to rest when the outside streets were giving you the worst approaches and ugly stares.

I wanted you to remember that love is a pair of arms you could fall on and sleep with.

LIFE AND ITS PERFECT IMPERFECTIONS

Oh, I see the beauty in shipwrecks.

I hear rhythms in waves.

And crystal stones I will surely collect.

Life is perfectly imperfect in its own ways.

Oh, I see stars when the lights are dim.

I see sparkles in the sky.

The bluish oceans are so enticing to swim.

Life is perfectly imperfect like rains that cry.

Oh, I see woods and falling leaves.

They scatter on the floor aesthetically.

The peace of the city at night is hard to believe.

Life is perfectly imperfect —live unapologetically.

Oh, I see friendship and empty coffee cups.

I hear laughter from people at a mere distance.

Excitements made the conversation jump.

Life is perfectly imperfect —take every chance.

Oh, I see empty streets and hallways.

Each has stories of fictional ghosts.

Stuff the hollows with dreams during the days.

Life is perfectly imperfect — live at your most.

Oh, I see empty parking lots and empty homes.

Plants outgrew and eeriness remains.

Each has a runaway story nobody knows.

Life is perfectly imperfect — live to the fullest

without having to explain

A PLACE

I always believe that it takes both hearts to keep the relationship going. You reminded me about the risks I took for you and how it was almost killing me. You reminded me that it takes both loves to maintain everything. I still remember how I loved you. I still remember how you used to love me like I was the only person that mattered to you. It was consoling to know that I could empty myself so you could be full of love.

For once, I found belongingness in you, I found a place in your embrace, and that's when I realized that I was capable of loving someone more than I could ever love anyone else. I saw myself ending with you and starting a family. I was so certain that I never think about life without you. I saw you and us until the end that was why I never hesitated to pour all the love that I had in my heart. I saw all the goodness in you and the way you loved me right before.

But then it was just me who see us in the future. It was just me who was left dreaming about us. You left as if you didn't break me. You left like I was nobody. Yet I forgive you. I keep forgiving you as if one day, you'll be back.

THROUGH MEMORIES

I still find myself smiling through the memories of how it all began. I still find myself wondering where I am going when I only had the memories of us to cling to. Is this keeping me company while I am trying to find a reason to forgive so I could forget those people that hurt me in the past? They said that we were too young to know about love, and we refused to believe them. But you see, despite how young our minds could get, we both knew that we can't force ourselves not to beat when it has already recognized happiness just by being with each other. You eradicated the hatred that I stored in my heart. There's no need for extravagant words or grand gestures —I knew since then that you will mean something to me.

We understood each other unexpectedly and in there, a genuine love blossomed. We started off realizing that being with each other is enough and there's no need to hop on wrong trains just to get their destinations. There, we saw how we felt comfortable in each other's company. We learned to enjoy each passing moment that we get. It was mutual —the feelings and affection. And I thank you for teaching my heart how to forgive. You taught me that the closest thing to healing is by forgiving first.

HUNDRED CHANCES

She still wanted to give him hundreds of chances. Still willing to stitch back the broken trust. She tried to forgive him again and again and still hold on to the slim chances that he will change for her again. It was cliché. But he never got tired of finding new ways to hurt her. She found again about how he's kindling fire with someone new. He got so excited at the thought of it that he didn't care if he was making new sets of alibis just to be with her.

He has so many women in his life, and she grew so exhausted fighting for a place that supposedly belonged to her. It was too much, and she didn't know if it's still worth losing herself because all she ever did was love him. She was so tired sobbing herself to sleep at night asking where she went wrong, what she doesn't have that he found in them, what she gave too much that he didn't like.

She wanted to let go, but she didn't want to let go of the probabilities that maybe one day, he will realize all the things he did to her.

She still hopes that soon, they will get the happiness that they once had. His love went astray, and she will always be the home he never got tired of abandoning. Somehow, despite it all, she's still willing to trust once again.

TRAITOR DESTINY

Our destiny clearly doesn't want us to be together. It's kind of difficult to know that there are hundreds of reasons for me to give up, but I chose not to because silently, I was hoping that you will too. I was silently praying that you will fight for the love that we thought was real, so we could make it sound right. But I guess, if you're meant to slip off from my grasp, there's nothing much I could do but to slowly watch you from afar, building a new life without me.

I wanted to make you know that no matter what happens, you will always have me. you will always have my hopes that would come alive every time I wished something for your success. You still have my dreams of you although I have to let go of my dreams for us. I will silently cheer you up and say your name like you're the best thing that has ever happened to me. I will speak your goals on behalf of you and will pray for them to become your reality. I will still love you although I must prepare myself for the truth that anytime soon, your heart will beat for someone else.

I will keep that slimmest hope and chance that it will be us in the end to reconnect broken lines, to reassemble broken promises, and to rewrite our plans through stars and sounds of waves.

JUST IN CASE

You still have me no matter what time of the day. No matter how hard the world would try to change the workings of your heart. I will be here to remind you that you have someone who wants nothing but just your happiness. I wanted you to live your life without worrying about who's hurting. I wanted you to take every chance that will give you reasons to be alive. I wanted you to chase your dreams and take all roads that will lead you closer to it. I want. And I hope that when things are okay when our hearts finally knew how to stand on certain grounds, we will find our way back to each other. I knew that when that day comes, it's still you that I will be choosing for. I hope you too. I hope it's still me. I hope it's not yet too late. I hope we could finally make 'us' happen.

Maybe our destiny will one day stop sounding so cruel and will give us another chance. So I will leave the doors to unlock.

I will leave my bedroom open. I will never silence my phone in case you'll call — in case you'll

*come back. In case you'll tell me you're fated to be
with me.*

TRUE LOVE

When you meet the right person, it's like everything that once a mess suddenly fell in the right place. It's like knowing your heart finally found a name it could beat on. Somehow, I'd like to believe that somewhere out there, someone is waiting for me to rearrange the scattered parts of his life and will thank me for being there.

The thought of it —excites me. The thought of it keeps me going. Probably because I knew that when the time is right I am thrilled since I knew the extent of the love I am capable of pouring. And that's the thing that makes me want to be in love with the idea of loving the right one and that all the grey clouds will part ways. All the years I spent waiting will be worth it.

Somehow, I believe that love will always be ready. There's no such thing as too early nor too late. There's always a part of us that would want to show the world how far you could go just to prove that you're prepared for what's to come. Somehow, for a long time, I believed that love will always stand out. It will always cross the lines —tangible or not. It will always burn the bridges. It will always understand, it will always be seen and heard by the heart. Somehow, I want to keep believing that love will find its way to be possible, to be reachable. I want to believe in love this way. I want to believe that true love is something that brings you peace.

WHAT IS PEACE?

Peace in such a way that we will get to experience the sense of adventure through spare time and reading creative word plays on our newly-discovered novel. Peace means being able to sleep at night without regretting yesterday. Peace means being able to sleep at night without having the fear of what will happen tomorrow. Peace means being able to understand that some mistakes are there to remind us that we have to learn something from it, and it is something about conditioning our hearts to fully embrace courage.

There I saw, that as I grew older, I only wanted peace of mind. No worries or if ever there is, I am able to surmount it. That's it and that's all.

PEACE OF MIND

As we grow old, we realized that we stopped running after the extravagance. We stopped hoping for having the massiveness of everything. We stopped hoping that there'll be more to what we already got. We stopped hoping that there's another ladder to climb on or gain more friends if we have to. We suddenly stopped hoping that all these greater things would give us the happiness that we ask for. Somehow, we realized that as we grew older, peace is the first and last thing we wanted to attain.

Peace in such a way that we will get to experience the sense of adventure through spare time and reading creative word plays on our newly-discovered novel. Peace means being able to sleep at night without regretting yesterday. Peace means being able to sleep at night without having the fear of what will happen tomorrow. Peace means being able to understand that some mistakes are there to remind us that we have to learn something from it, and it is something about conditioning our hearts to fully embrace courage.

There I saw, that as I grew older, I only wanted peace of mind. No worries or if ever there is, I am able to surmount it. That's it and that's all.

SAME MOMENT

And she believes that true love means providing that someone the peace that they deserve even if it calls for her to vacate the picture. She pondered that to enable her to give him peace; she must let her go first. She realized that there are hundreds of reasons why she should give up but she keeps holding on to the smallest hint of hope. There, she realized that she must let go of her grip on the memories that are too impossible to repeat again. So slowly, she started letting each detail go, she started giving him the peace that he craves for. He started hoping there are better ways to free him where she's no longer mandated to endure pain.

There, she felt the bullets of reality striking all her soft parts. She wanted to grant him the peace that he's been asking for. She wanted him to remember her as someone who loved him unconditionally.

So slowly, she vanished. Slowly, she took her steps one at a time until she finally steps out from the circumference of her wishful thinking. And later on, she realized that pain redirected her to see life through a different lens.

She also found peace the same moment she gave him that.

UNTIL MY HEART KNOWS

Trust is such a fragile thing to break. So fragile that it'll never be the same again once it is broken. And maybe I will forever carry this because sometimes, my scars remained with me forever. They reassemble a past that has so much grudge to hold, so much pain that peeks in, so much betrayal that still lingered time after time. I know one day I will be able to forgive and accept that things already happened. There'll be a day when I'll start getting up from my own feet and start all over again.

And I could no longer change what was changing; I could no longer hope to undo the past. I just know that things will soften one day and that days will be brighter than now but I will take all the time that I need to heal. I have to begin with myself. I will one day forgive and trust once again but this time, it'll be with different people, and I pray for myself that as soon as I learn to accept all versions of defenses, everything will go down the drain as well.

Pray for me that time will heal me so I could accept and forgive.

Until my heart knows how to trust again.

WARS INSIDE

Wars, don't just exist on the battlefield. They don't always indicate bombs, or guns, or any sort of physical terror. Some wars exist in the mind of a person. The wars that take over the peace that was supposed to sway us when the wind blows so harshly. The wars that we have inside us will surely make us feel less alive, feel less valued, feel less appreciated. Somehow, it erases every stain of happiness in our skin and makes us think that every day is a battle between negativities and self-loathe.

Somehow, peace is more like a star in the night sky that we yearned to reach someday to put inside our room so it could shed a little light sometimes. Peace is more like a long-forgotten favorite song that we wish will play when we badly needed evidence of our past happy self. Peace is more like a poem whose rhymes consoles your souls, whose meaning goes deep in the bones. We knew peace before war. And we wanted to regain it once again when we go through the saddest chapter of our lives where we have to surrender our little flags.

I hope despite all the wars we have to face, peace will prevail.

REPAIRED

I tried to sew back every crumbling trust. I tried to comprehend every broken edge to where our silence could lead us. I tried to unstiffen all the shrill words hoping that it won't hurt the same anymore the second time around. I tried my best to pull you back every time I feel that you're taking your phases away from me. It wasn't me because that's something that I never truly do in my past relationships but for you, I absorbed my pride and stood next to your towering conviction. I never paused to remind you about the memories we had hope that they will be enough to make you think that I am worth staying and fighting for.

Maybe being with you and showing you how you became my world spoiled you and that you took me for granted because you know that I will always forgive. I will always ignore my pain just to forget the ugly past. You always knew that I love you more than you love me and that you stayed with me because you know you will be needing someone who will be there when you finally got nobody.

And it's tiring to put trust back again into its shape knowing that anytime soon, you'll shatter it again.

WHEN IT COMES TO YOU

How was I able to hate someone for choosing his happiness even if it meant he had to break me that much? I know time could change people, and sadly it changed you. Suddenly you became a stranger to me, a stranger that held both my harshest and weakest sides. You became a stranger whose name still gives me pangs of pain, where every little thing you did was directing to pierce my heart. You started breaking me like it was your habit. You started hurting me as if it was part of your agenda. All of a sudden, you forgot the way you used to love me, and now, you're taking every power you have to continuously take me for granted and shatter the parts of me that are within your reach.

I want to know why you have to break me when all I ever did was forgive you for your past mistakes. I wonder why you have to hurt me when all I ever did was stitch you back to your old self so you could start all over again. You always leave when you get a chance to do so.

And come back as if I was a refugee of your lost torn self. You always hurt me over and over and over again as if it was the easiest thing to do. You hurt me because you know that when it comes to you, I will always forgive.

HOW

If there was one thing that I wished I could skip, it would be no other than the echoes of betrayals that remained beside me. The never-ending sting of the past that did nothing but drown me constantly on my self-blames and palpable errors.

These ghosts stayed with me when the rest of the world expected me to move on from it and accept that it already happened. It happened when the trust that you built so delicately was torn down by someone you least expected, and all you could do was watch it scatter on your floor like broken glass. It just hurts. It just hurts so bad that you convinced yourself not to forgive anymore. You just stared at it, too hesitant to clean it instantly because you know that the moment you touch it, it will just give you cuts. And forgiveness was something that you shut away from your life. They all stayed, and no matter how much you try to put them back, the cracks will remind you that nothing comes in perfect shape again. Nothing.

So tell me how do we forgive something or someone we don't truly understand?

IN HOPE OF SURVIVAL

I never knew that this is what emptiness felt like —no matter how much I tried, I could never fill up the void I had within my chest. It was just too much. It was just too heavy. It was just too tiring. I would like to understand where this pain came from, but I didn't know which part of the page I should start. I don't know which word fits perfectly with what I truly feel. It feels like I had been pierced with so many versions of past mistakes that I made home in my flesh and took residence inside my head.

The darkness of all the blames I heard from the past kept on taunting me to recall them. I somehow got used to this. That when someone hurts me, I hated myself instead of hating the person who gave me nothing but aches in return. When someone lies to me, I blame myself for not knowing better, for being so soft, for being so trusting, and for being too much and less at the same time.

Up until these days, survival sounded so jargon.

Up until now, I still hope I'll survive the nights to battle another morning tomorrow.

TOWARDS FORGIVENESS

I recall the days where everything that happened to me in the past was once the high tides and reckless lightning that I need to face. All the errors in my code reminded me about how unworthy I was as a person. It keeps breaking me apart and I knew it was so hard to emerge when the world's weight has stopped me from rising up. I drowned there. I sunk. I was buried. I was forgotten.

Despite all that, I kept them inside me. I tried to conceal these and hid them away from everyone. I needed to hide these just as much as possible because I was afraid that I would make higher fatalities when the time comes that my bottled up emotions would explode. I knew I should never tell anyone about this —including the one who loved me.

I hid this behind the empty sheets of a forgotten diary and shoved this underneath the carpet. I pushed them further although I know they knew their way back to me. All these disappointments that other people emphasized. All these words reassembled like sharp knives that I slush on my skin. I remember all of them. And it's nice to know that somehow, I made it.

ONE DAY

All these triggers I keep pulling and all these floods I created when my tears began pouring must all be suffered by only myself—just me and not anyone who made me this.

I wanted to hold onto my pieces, but every time I do, the more they crumbled, the more I tore down, and the more I stopped wanting to try again. I was just too tired to understand why out of all the people, I became the unluckiest one. I found it hard to let go of the voices of the people who lied to me, from the touches of hands that spell out deceit. I hate the way I stared with loathing at the person that I see in front of the mirror. I was betrayed. After all, I was weak because I couldn't pluck up the courage to fight for myself, and the funniest part was that I was aware. I was entirely aware, yet I couldn't even do something to save myself. I kept saving them even if it meant I would kill myself in the process. I kept losing myself on times when I was desperate to find my way back to life, but there I was, still lost in every step that I take.

I still hope one day, I'll survive the roughest patch I was on.

I MUST

My history already drained me. I was completely empty that I consumed all my time overthinking about everything until bled enough to death. I was not myself anymore. It really took time. I really needed to feel all shreds of disloyalty. Each day that I get to wake up to, I tend to uncover something that would only hurt me more. All these infidelities. I wonder what else I didn't know. I wonder how many secrets I was about to know that would slash a little death on my wrist.

I realized that life, after all, was not just about breathing in front of everyone. I realized that life was not just about forgiving them for hurting me. It's not just about me understanding that I was another body made up of mistakes or the weaknesses people took with to betray me. I hated everything that I went through, things I was going through, and so as the ones I had to face. I never liked how my heart and mind never learned to be friends. I hated myself day after day. I hated the fact that I could never hate the world for hurting me this much.

I hated everything that's happening around me. But I needed to survive all these.

I have to. I need to. I must.

WORST DAYS

It's nice to have someone who will arrive at the most unexpected time of your life: the day where you needed saving the most. You have come to my life to love me and to stay with me because you also needed my love for you. You helped me get up from my fall. I hope that we will never get tired of being each other's go-to person. You are the only person I trust with all of my life, the only person who knows me better than anyone. You will always be the man I will forever thank God for having, for being here with me.

We still have more years to count and that means we still have more memories waiting to happen. We still have more travels to pursue. We still have more stories to share, more coffees to share, more secrets to spill, and assurances of being kept behind the closet. We still have more happiness waiting for us to grab it. And I hope that there still be a heart that is willing to explain and another heart that will be open to listening. I want us to be more mature, more secure, more in love.

Thank you for knocking and reminding me that I could always survive the worst days.

BROKEN TRUST

When trust is broken, I wonder if I can put them back together again like nothing happened. I didn't know what to do. Every morning was just too dark for me to function; every night, I drink myself to sleep, so the sober sadness will remain unwelcomed. Every happy memory that I keep with me is now dressed in doubts, in unanswered questions, and in sincere wonderings. I no longer know which true and genuine.

The darkness of all the blames I heard from the past keeps on taunting me to recall them. Sometimes, I dont know where to run. I am afraid that if ever I did, I would find a place for comfort, a place where I can be in when I need an escape. I am afraid to be attached to it, to get used to it only to realize that I am not allowed to call it my home. I am trying to hold back from giving my all because I am terrified that not everyone will stay with me during turbulent storms. It's just too hefty that even happiness is just too far from my reach. Somehow,

I'm afraid to trust again not because I can but because I know they may break it again.

CHALLENGE

Since the beginning, I could hear all the murmurs about you. They warned me about you, but still, you convinced me that I should only trust you. I should trust my heart, so I could trust your words. They kept repeating everything bad about you and that I should keep my way out before I welcome the potential damages that will spell out your name. They reminded me about your mistakes and that I should never allow you to create new ones with me. It was too much for me to process, but then, it was you who I believed in.

Maybe I heard all these warnings; all of them trying to give me a word how I should never let myself in your lines because once I did, there'll be no other way out. But there's something in you that was just too irresistible: something that softens my hard heart. In an instant, everything they said about you was shoved on to my oblivion. Right there, I stopped myself from believing them.

And I have grown to love those mysteries in you.

I took the challenge of loving you and told myself that you're worth a try. I trusted myself enough to trust you.

STAY KIND

People face different battles every day. The one you're facing right now might have dealt with the same monsters inside her head that she hadn't defeated yet. Some have stories they don't dare to share, so they keep it inside their heart only to realize that they were nothing but an atomic bomb waiting to explode. Some have secrets that they want to keep behind their drawers, storms that they can't tame, storms that they can't name. They still have it hoping one day, they will all pass.

Others have problems they prefer to keep inside their diaries; all the hints were unread and all cries of help are never heard. Some have their own cliff to jump from but are waiting for a sign not to. Everyone begs for survival, for a living, for having a clearer purpose when it comes to existence, so be kind. Stay kind, and never judge anyone by the problems they go through. Never stop them from feeling something real. Don't push them down the waters until they drown just because you can't keep them afloat.

Allow them to heal; the least that we could do is to stay kind. Just be kind.

YOUR KINDNESS

I must be honest, the more I know you the more I appreciate the little things that made you who you are now. Silently, I am observing some of the many features that I really admire from you. Little do you know but you are actually the cutest when you complain when you hate the traffic jam because you hate getting stuck in between and wasting your time there. Your sweet tooth, how chocolates were enough to lighten up your mood, you like kids so much and that somehow shows your kindness and your softness. You like art, you like the meaning behind the museum, the secrets behind the displays. You are made for art, you have a heart for art, so as for me, you are my favorite work of art.

You are a strong person that taunts my weaknesses. It's challenging me, but I realize I am becoming a better person because of you. I defied my patience because I know every hard work will be worth it in the end. I am not in a hurry. I am not putting all the pressure on you. Take all of the time that you need. I just want to guarantee that you will always have this one person that will forever adore you and that includes your goodness and flaws. I will forever be here. *Never forget that I fell in love with your kindness.*

YOUR GOOD HEART

I have known you by heart and that's the thing that matters most. You made me think that I didn't need a crowd to comfort me but just a few goods and sincere people like you. Your kindness taught me to accept life and how it'll never get along with me sometimes. You opened the door without hesitation. You always spoke the words I never thought I needed and always makes me feel at ease. You always put us first and set aside your personal struggles just to be with us when we needed you the most.

I write this letter to let you know that you will also have the best support system that you needed in me. Your kindness is my inspiration. The kind that made me realize that it's completely okay to break in. I will always be here for you doing things the same way you did to me not for the reciprocal obligation but because I know you are worthy of affection and loyal friendship. I will always pick your call no *matter what time of the day or night it could be. I will always embrace your sadness when you can't take it anymore.*

I will always use your kindness to us as a reason for me to be kind to everyone I meet.

HERE

I'll always admire you and your kindness. I will always remind you that you are completely different from everyone that I've met. I will always understand the cynical inside jokes that you can't burst out, and I will always laugh along with you. I will always assure you that even if the world will give up on you which seems to be rather impossible, I will always stay here with you and will always admire you because I know you the most. I will always make you feel that you're too much of that right person that the universe should protect at all costs. You're so exceptional —so raw.

You're indeed close to perfection because you're more than just a pretty skin but you have the biggest heart. Thank you so much for staying and for being here with me. I will always be here for you as well. I will forever recall all the big and small things that you did out of love and kindness and how it made me embrace the entity of life. We could always lean on, stay, and be inspired by the friendship that we have.

I am always and will always be here for you. Remember that.

SOME CHANCES

I have always been reckless with my actions, probably because I thought you'll give me every opportunity to learn from my mistakes. I knew I let my imperfections justify my errors and never did anything to lessen it. I kept losing every opportunity that you gave me. For so long, I grew so confident that I could make anyone stay without even trying. I always believed that life would give me everything that I deserved no matter how many times I took it for granted, no matter how much I tried to overuse the power that I had on someone who gave me a heart and love to keep. I used to believe in that until the day I met you, until the day you trusted me your love. Not until the same moment that I broke it so evenly.

I must admit that I wasn't the most faithful one. I overused the chance; I abused the opportunity that you have given me. I guess that was because I was at ease with the freshness of our relationship and every memory will be filling the surfaces only.

I thought I'll lose nothing and no one if I'll betray a little trust. You are different from anyone that I got to know before and losing you now made me realize that some chances are gone forever.

HIS LOST OPPORTUNITY

Her doors were closed. She's no longer giving him another shot of opportunity to be used against her.

It was the kind of heartache that he knew he deserved, yet he wished for the universe to give him a chance to straighten what he did. He was never given the chance to explain his sincerity. She turned off everything even the slimmest hope that was left in him. He was hurt knowing he mattered less to her anymore and that he was never given the opportunity to double his efforts until he could make up for his errors.

He knew he hurt her, and he will never take it away from her. She has the right to hate him and his actions. She was allowed to despise how he hurt her and everything that he kept everything behind her back. She was allowed to storm out and to hurt him the same way he did to her. He would accept everything and he would never stop her from inflicting him the same density of pain. He wished that he could still have the guarantee of having her again despite what happened.

He still wanted to hold her. He still wanted to see that smile on her face.

He still wanted to be the reason behind her laughter. Just one more moment. Just one more try. Just one more opportunity to make things right.

DRIFTED OPPORTUNITIES

He still wants to be the first person she remembers first thing in the morning and end the night with. He still wants to be the one who'll get to hear your good news and the one who will understand why she had a ruined day. He still wishes he could get the chance to hear her childhood stories and the tales behind her scars. He still wants to be there in her life. He still wants her to want him.

It hurts how she made up her mind so abruptly and took leaving as the last resort. The opportunity to start all over again was never given to him. He knows everything he did will give her nightmares, too, but she has always been strong enough to conquer her sadness. His mistakes leave her with cuts that an apology couldn't mend. He gave her reasons to be insecure and intimidated. He knows she will begin to ponder which part of him was true and which was fabricated, which part of their memories was real and which was not. He broke his own self in front of her, and she was certain that she will never see him the same way she did.

Breaking her trust means breaking everything she believed in them, and he could never put them back again the same way it was. Nothing seemed possible to him right now everything was nothing but just drifting opportunities.

KNOCK ONCE MORE

He regretted everything. He regretted the opportunities she gave him that he took for granted because he thought she'll give him more. If only he was capable of flipping the hourglass and change what he did. If only he saw them fall apart because of it, he wished he did something better, and perhaps, it would've saved them. He's still hurt, but he wasn't sure if it was valid knowing he suffered the consequences of his own actions. It was a pain that he felt right to feel. He knows he hurt her worse, and she's still breaking herself from the way he shattered her. He wanted to fight for the place that he once had in her life, so he was begged for one more chance. He was begging her to allow him to take the pain he gave to her recklessly, to allow him to give her everything he never gave her.

He can't imagine someone being there with her, fetching her, and having dinner with her. He still wants it to be him. He still wants it to be them.

He still wishes he can change her mind. He still wishes for opportunity to knock once more.

THANKS

It was weird how time moved so slowly and the rest of the world moved on. The moment we began relighting old memories back to life like a rare opportunity that we have to grab with bravery or else, we'll lose it forever. It somehow felt like you were mine yesterday. I realize it was the kind of happiness that was incomparable. It was real back then; it's just we're too young for it. We didn't realize that we enjoyed each other's company to the point that our conversations grew longer and deeper. It was at the moment where my heart recognizes love again. It was the moment that I realized that I was ready to fall in love again. I was ready to fall for you again. It was the time in between our separation that made me realize how massive the happiness that I allowed time and fate to take away from me. With that moment, I wanted to make up for the memories that never really died inside me at all.

We tried reconnecting dots until it all led to the chances of us. Tried so hard to use each split second to this opportunity to start again. Both of us chased that possibility and took the risk. I was the happiest because again; you're my answered prayer. It was like I finally found a place in this world that would love me not just for my good days but also for my bad days.

We learned from it. We wanted to make it as a reason why we should learn from it.

I wanted to thank you for giving me a chance. This opportunity would never be wasted. I wanted to thank you for giving me a reason to learn and grow.

"Spring: a lovely reminder of
how beautiful change can truly be."
—Unknown

Summertime Blues

"Let my summertime blues be the sky,
the sea, and your eyes..."
—Hasmita Verma

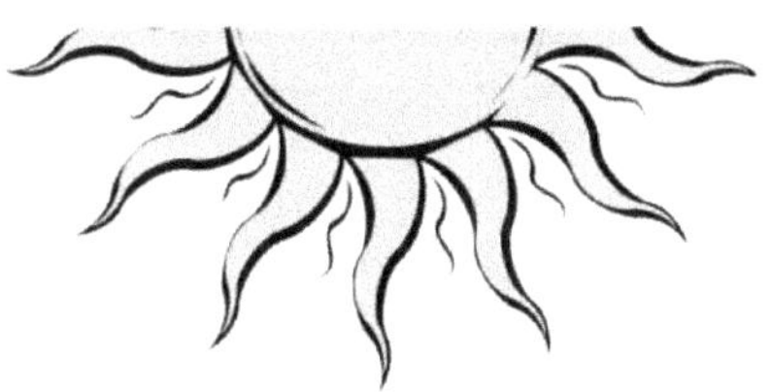

EXPLORING ONESELF

We always search for something.
We want to know what might happen after spring.
We want to know where else we could go with these wings.
Or if there's more meaning to the songs we sing.

We always wonder what tomorrow brings.
We think about who holds the other end of the string.
We want to know what lingers when the lights blink.
And want to understand why the past still clings.

We want to count how long until the rain stops pouring.
We want to know what comes after the morning.
We want to understand why there was darkness in the evenings.
And why sadness comes without a little warning.

We want to know what's behind the walls.
We want to extend some unexpected phone calls.

We want to explore ourselves including our weaknesses and flaws.
We want to know us even more through our rights and wrongs.

We explore so many things, past and present.
We try to understand the tales behind the unpleasant.
We want to explore even when the moon is crescent.
We aim to fight like it's the future scent.

When will we take the courage to explore ourselves?
We left the parts of us aside like forgotten books on shelves.
We were terrified to see our imperfections, too afraid to delve.
So we refused to accept who we are, self-doubts never heave.

START AGAIN

They always said, there's still life after death. We could be reincarnated and start again. I'd like to believe in it because it gives me a new face of hope that if ever we didn't make it, then maybe we could in the next lifetime. I want to believe that even if the world will not give me a chance to have the things that I had been fantasizing about, or dreaming about when I am asleep, maybe I could finally have them in the next life.

There, I saw how I finally learned to give u when nothing seemed to work the way I wanted it. I wanted to believe that there's definitely a better purpose to let go of some of my dreams that I can't seem to put into a whole picture. Maybe I will have them someday when I am finally reincarnated. Maybe I will have a brand-new fate where I'll be luckier, or less dismayed.

I wanted to see the idea of reincarnation as another way of believing that I will soon have everything I wished for. It may not work out now, but I am sure that it will be in the future. Maybe this life is not just for me.

FAMILIARITY

I think I saw you before, my heart is telling me something and it was like we've met a long long time ago. We met in a way that only my heart remembers. Your eyes reassemble the ocean that drowns me when I stare too long. Your words were perfectly stitched into paragraphs that make my heart flutter. Your voice was soothing to my bones that nobody else has ever done to me before. It was simple, yet it was real. I felt like I have known you before. I would watch you move; every single step reminds me of something that I have already forgotten. Does it mean that you are my soul mate and that we have met you before and now, after being reincarnated, the universe paved the way again so we could meet again?

Is this even possible to feel something truly familiar especially with how you made me feel so alive with your presence? It's surreal how one person could make me go out of my usual thoughts. You made me ponder that maybe we were meant for each other —before and even now.

And maybe, if we didn't make it in this time, we will meet again in another lifetime. Maybe we'll always find a way to bump each other's path.

FEAR

The footsteps were getting louder, telling me it's getting closer. I would cover myself under my blanket, my young fragile self was so scared. I would cover myself with bravery but was too terrified to open my eyes. I was afraid of what's there sitting at the edge of my bed, I was afraid to check who's staring at me when I have nothing but just a weak heart beating in me and a constrained scream inside my head that I can't even let out.

Sometimes, I could feel it lingering inside my room, wandering every corner, and making sure that I could feel its presence. Even if I shut my eyes so tightly, I could feel it breathing so close to my ears. I could feel its coldness filling in the spaces.

And I grew so terrified towards the unknown. The shadows were lurking; the intangibles were urging to be disheveled. I grew so scared about what I had never seen. I was so afraid that it will occupy my entire being and stop trusting darkness.

IN CHASE OF LIFE

Have you been to different places?

Where everyone you see has unfamiliar faces?

Where languages spoken become unfamiliar phrases?

It gives you a thrill as your heart races.

You walk with bravery and eagerness on new streets.

You take a quick snack on sidewalk seats.

You pay bills at convenience stores and kept the receipts.

You knew life is a quest, it makes you feel complete.

Have you sailed on different boats?

Have you felt the water below as the boat float?

Have you been to places that were remote?

Can you recall how you journeyed in that route?

Have you ever felt the comfort of new regions?

Have you found it on the streets or in museums?

Have you felt the urge to pray on cathedrals that are not your religion?

Have you regretted every single plan you made, as well as your decisions?

Have you been somewhere that made you feel more alive?
Have you woken up feeling more motivated to thrive?
Have you been into roads that call for an endless drive?
Have you ever seen scenic things that make you want to try and survive?

Have you finally seen the essence of taking a journey?
Have you found yourself in that quest, every second is worthy.
Has it made you feel like you need to be in a hurry?
That alone would make you feel alive, so there's no need to worry.

BEST PARENTS

As I grew up, I realized a lot of things. I realized that I need to heal myself from the twisted family tale that haunted me for years. I told myself that I will never let my children go through the same pain and develop abandonment issues within themselves. I wanted them to grow up with parents that don't only show affection in front of them. I will marry a man who will love me as much as I love him. I will try my hardest to search for a one-woman-man who will not leave me morning poisons and deception.

I want to give my future family the happiness that I never got when I started growing up. I will make them feel that their parents are the most excited people who'll get to hear both good and bad news first above anything else. I want them to grow up with nothing to carry with them. I will love them and I will make sure that the person I tied the knot with will become so in love with them that he will no longer search for this value in someone else.

I will love him the same way he wanted to be loved. So we could give our children the best life they'll be thankful for having.

NOT GOOD ENOUGH

There were moments when I feel like I was never good enough. I would spend the rest of my life wanting to do something but too terrified when it's finally near me. it's like an irony to want something so bad but too afraid when it's finally within your reach. I was too terrified to give it a go because the consequences sometimes overpower me.

Somehow, there were silent days when I told myself I should break free from all the doubts that I had accumulated throughout my weak days. I wanted to get out from this oppression that I ruled to myself —the low confidence and the lack of trust that I could do something and not mess up.

I wanted to give it a try, but the doubts left an echo inside my head that reduces my esteem. I watched my doubts swallow that little optimism until I was left there on the floor —drained and regretful. I just wanted to do something for myself but my fears are always taking a step forward and I would slow down my steps and watch my reservations take over my entire body.

And in there, I will spend a long time trying to understand the opportunities that I almost had — opportunities that I lost. I will think about it until I began hating myself.

LOVE IS LOVE

Years have passed, and he still loves him —his one great love. For some reason, they knew it was real somehow. They loved each other so dearly although it was just them who gets know it. They were so in love with each other that they thought they could conquer all the contradictions and judgments. But they were wrong, people's opinions held so much power that it became a reason for them to lose each other.

They parted ways but at some point, their hearts still recognize the love that they think they deserve. The kind of true love that they found with each other. Years later, they met again unexpectedly. The feelings that they reserved started rattling inside their chests — their hearts still recognize each other. The heart never forgets the love that was supposed to be happy if only they never allowed the crowd to tell them how it should beat. But they knew it's all too late.

And this is the thing about love — it knows no boundary. It knows no rules. It knows nothing but just real things. Love is love. Some get the happy endings, others don't.

GIVE AND TAKE

There'll be days where you won't have much.
Days where blessings don't come in rush.
There'll be moments where blessings don't come in
a bunch.
And signs of graces hadn't reached your touch.

There'll be nights where you'll feel empty.
Nights where you didn't have plenty.
There'll be chances that didn't have entry.
But despite all that, just wait gently.

On toughest moments like that,
Remember the people who gave you a pat.
Those who shared their knowledge— close to a
fact.
Those who left your life with generous impact.

Remember the people who shared you their
blessings.
People who guided you on your dwellings.
Those who shared a light when you're dealing with
the setting.

Those who gave you wonderful starts after the endings.

When your life turned a little better.
Remember the ones who gave without measures.
They shared words until problems weighted like feathers.
And on rainy afternoons, they shared with you their shelters.

Make them feel remembered.
People who put merry in December.
Those who puzzled you together.
And shared with you the courage you'll bring with you forever.

RESPECT THEM

Respect the people who choose to follow a path that nobody else has taken too. You have no idea how it took her so many times to ponder on it, the endless cycle of constant consequences one should take if ever that choice went wrong.

Respect the people who choose to step out from any toxic circle even if it means they have to start living alone. You will never know how it took them so much to lose just so they could begin again with themselves. You will never know how they felt so lost while being surrounded by unworthy people and superficial outbursts of laugher.

Respect the one who decided to come out from their long-locked closet. Respect them for choosing to be themselves even if they knew they will never get the approval or acceptance from everyone they asked for it. Respect their courageousness for not everyone has it to carry the weight of words.

Respect people who decided to just be happy even if it means they have to turn their backs away from the life they grew so sick of living. Respect their choices, their aspirations. Respect how they wanted to give themselves another chance to be truly alive and happy while it's not too late yet.

ONE DAY

I knew I will regret this one day. I know that it will take my sanity away from me. I know it'll exhaust me just by thinking about it. But then again, I'll still give it a massive try.

I will disconnect from everyone who started to trench my energy to see the goodness in me. I will begin with those who only like me because they see something in me that they could take. I will also walk away from those who keep bringing back to life the mistakes that I buried ten meters below. I will stay out from those who did nothing but to compare me to anyone better than me and gives me the alarm that I should wake up to the sad truth that I will never be the person who could exceed them.

I will never give them a reason why I am suddenly out of reach. I will never tell them why I don't want them in my life anymore. I will never allow them to step back when they started telling me they miss me.

And I knew I will regret this someday but the consequences of staying away from those who did nothing good to me will always be bearable. I will only regret it if I stay here and lose myself in their worthlessness.

YOU ARE FREE TO GO

Maybe you set up the standard and that you will be this someone that I will smile if I remembered in my future. Someone I would gladly create a story to tell everyone with. You will be this someone who will always give me the best memories about how crazy and surreal love could be. How one-sided love could be so cruel and yet acceptable. I wanted to love you still because that's the thing that brings me joy now. Those are the things that broke so many of my bricked walls with. Loving you became the reason why I wrecked my fences with, why I leave my telephone line open and why I always wanted to be on my finest shots. I will still have so many reasons why I am thankful for meeting someone who showed me both the saturation and hues of love and how to widen my acceptance to the things that don't do along my way.

I just want you to know that nothing is pushing you to love someone like me who only fantasizes about someone out of my track. I just want you to know that I am completely okay with everything that I have and everything that I didn't have. The love that I have that I will never hesitate to give you and the love that you could never payback. I swear things are fine and you are free to choose someone who made you feel things —the one that you made me feel.

SET YOURSELF FREE

Set yourself free, learn to take a risk.

Do not think of anything brisk.

Just do the things that you think.

Since not all sails will sink.

Set yourself free, let go of your fears.

Do not be afraid to shed a tear.

Your happiness will soon appear,

Just see the beauty of life, sharp and sheer.

Set yourself free, do what you want.

Do not cling to an ending, you could always start.

You could stay up until sunrise, just watch.

Experiences will absolutely make you smart.

Set yourself free from the terrors of the past.

Bring your imperfections with you and all the contrasts.

You must not be afraid about how the unknown shadow casts.

Believe me, no darkness stays or lasts.

Set yourself free from all the cuts and scars.

Do not be terrified that you won't reach the stars.

All these ugly memories will fade like passing cars.

And you will soon wake up with bliss like alarms.

Set yourself free from other's opinions of you.

You deserve to see the sun's perfect saturations and hues.

You deserve to start into something rare and new.

Just set yourself free from the feelings of being blue.

LET THEM KNOW THAT YOU KNOW

It's hard to find a balance in this world. There's always an up, and there's always a down. People who are in the position are always looking down on those they could abuse. They overuse the power that they have until it turns into violence and abuse. We are enslaved by people who are in higher offices, wishing that their commands will be obeyed and sang like a national anthem. They look up to themselves way too much that they thought everyone they get to meet will bow to them.

So tell them what you have seen. Tell them what you have observed. Tell them what you know. Shake their conscience. Impose the truth, so the crowd will know. Let them know that someone's watching over them. Make them feel that they are watched, that not everyone in their scope is ignorant.

Show to them that you're keeping an eye on them and that enslaving us has to end. Wake their fears. Threaten their threats. Never be enforced to shut down when their ego was too high and demanding. Speak up for your rights. Encourage people to read between the lines and to see how being well-informed will free you from the abuse that's happening around them.

REASON TO KEEP LIVING

May your youth be filled with good people who will carve you towards remembering the importance of having good values, of being brave enough to pursue what you really wanted to become. May you be surrounded by people who allow you to grow based on your ways, but at the same time, will guide you so you won't go astray in case you wanted to cross some delimited lines. May you see the happiness that will stay with you and will make you understand that it's not a perfect life but you will learn through your mistakes.

You will get up once you fall down. You will remember what made you want to be strong. You will recall all these people who let you down but you will thank them later for you used them as your inspiration. May you be filled with so much joy during your youth that you will no longer open up a space for the darkness to consume. May you be with good people who will introduce you to arts and literature. People who will help you cope with the things that you find hard to start with.

May your youth bring you a reason to keep living. May your happiness back then be resurrected — enough to overwhelm your today's trauma and will just leave you alone.

NO HOPE

This is to all the things that we don't know.

It's hard to be involved in the pleasure of satisfaction even if the only way you could have it is by doing a wrong thing. We commit a crime for we thought it is the easiest and fastest way of gaining something without exerting hard work. When greed overcomes the heart, compassion and kindness suddenly subsided the body. We forget to be appreciative of small things because we ran after the most expensive things your bank account could afford. Even if it means you have to slip some money in your pocket although it doesn't belong to you.

You allowed the whispers of temptation to leave the moral values that were instilled in you. You wanted to get everything you could. You wanted to show the world your supremacy. You wanted to be at the top so you'll be praised. You are taken solely by those who are only valued by society. You wanted to blend with the blinding colors of the world's elite people. You bring the best in you by stealing what belongs to the masses. You wanted to bring yourself the extravagance but your heart has been covered by greediness. If that's the majority of people in places that we live in — there'll be no hope for a change.

ACHIEVED

It all happened when I was little.

I always settled for being in the middle.

I would memorize rules like a riddle.

And watch all the chances fade like ripples.

When I was young, I was shrinking from the rest.

I was never at my fair best.

In every event, I was never a special guest.

Like I was another dry petal on pages that they pressed,

That when I learned to set up a goal.

This time, I will feed happiness to my soul.

I will not take my self-doubts to take control.

I am my own best character; I know my role.

I learned to dream big and real.

I made bad choices, and the consequences I make a deal.

Despite all that, I learned to understand what I feel.

I need to grow. I need to heal.

I started envisioning victories.
Big or small, they never give me reason for my miseries.
I will be better, enough to make good histories.
I will suggest and soon, the world will agree.

Soon, the world will hear.
Soon, everyone would give me their ears.
Reaching my goals is the only thing I see clear.
I know I could make it possible, dear.

FAILED

We failed to do these things.

One, we always wanted to rely upon our expectations to an answered prayer. We waited for it to be heard but most of us refuse to believe who will grant it.

When we speak, we always wanted to own the spotlight. We eat the entire running time, we make sure every word we share is noted and remembered. We wanted to sound larger than anyone who sits on the audience corner but none of us had the ethic to listen to suggestions, to their concerns and own take.

When we spend, we refuse to acknowledge how useful it could be. How far it could serve us right. We failed to ask ourselves if it's really important so we expend to temporary bliss. We disburse on small things that result in bigger amounts when calculated together. We find it easy to spend on nonsensical things but find it too hard to save from what we earn.

We always take the option of quitting. As we failed on the first try, we downgrade ourselves and settle on the sloop of embarrassment. We never hesitated to quit and refused to see how much we improved from it to give ourselves another chance to try.

We always wanted to receive all the good things in life but failed to ask ourselves if we are good enough as a person.

SMALL VOICE

Ever since I was a kid, there's always a small voice inside my head that keeps me guided when making decisions about my life. I wanted to know something I wasn't sure of, and believe myself enough that I could handle it may it be a good or bad outcome. I always listen to what my thoughts were saying, may it be about people, about places I wanted to move in, about aspirations I want to dash when the time is finally right.

I am always thirsty for knowledge about knowing — of discovering more about the unknown, about what's not yet happening. I want to try things my instinct is telling me to do, to follow, or to pursue. Because I knew life's too short and people's words are always misleading. I don't want to waste my time holding on to grudges when people failed to reach my anticipations. So I will hold onto my own instincts, to my own beliefs and thoughts. I will hold on to where my intuition is taking me for it never failed me once. I want to believe in something wonderful and unregretful.

I want to live my life on my own terms without worrying about whom I am going to share it with. I trust myself in this.

SCARS

I still have them — the scars they said that will one day turn into stars. I still have them on my skin. It hurts during the day. It still hurts during the night. It aches every time I try to heal them and hurts the same when I leave it all alone. They reminded me about the past that I was never truly got over. I fantasized about the day where my anxiety will just start to leave me like how easy it is for others to abandon me.

I want to imagine myself finally free from this dusk I was stuck for years but over time it tries, I realized I was so weak to even turn the knob of the door. The scars, all the parallels and horizontals on my wrist, resemble my story that's too painful to retell. Everything around me gives me a reason to be scared. Everything in me always hurts days after the day I wonder if others feel the same way too or is it just me?

I never thought that I built my wall way too high I don't know what it was really for. Was it to keep me out from all these people or was it just me who wanted to keep them away from me?

WANDERING GHOST

There were restless nights that hold me completely apart. I would sit there and think that maybe, that's how I should face life after death —a wandering ghost. The day I died was also the day that made me realize that there's more to people's emotions and how they deal with the death of others.

I saw people who were so close to me still shedding a tear and refuse to accept the reality that I was already not part of the world. I saw most of my friends staring at my casket with disbelief in their eyes. I saw how they speak with my name with so much gentleness, like a delicate glass that keeps breaking. I saw people who used to take me for granted to refused to answer back when I needed help being there. I saw how they mourned with pretension and cried because everyone else was doing it.

I saw Mama sitting on the front pew, still looking at me like all the flowers stands surrounding me — slowly but surely withering. I saw how she ran out of tears, saw how she said she's still dreaming. And it aches me into my deepest core. It burns me to think they were all unprepared to lose me and that's the hardest part because just as much as I thought I could —still, I was never ready to leave.

SUDDEN LOSS

I still think about us —even after nine years, I could still recall everything like it was just yesterday. You were the only person that I loved that much and at the same time, the only person I grew to memorize with. Within those nine years, I tried to convince myself to let go. I saw myself fail from moving forward.

I sculpted the ghost of the past and walked on a ghost town filled with clinging hopes that maybe we will meet again, and we will try once more. I named all these ghosts after your dreams, how you wished to build a two-story house someday. I named all these ghosts after your failures — failures that witnessed. I named all of these ghosts after how stood up, how I saw you get up from being stumbled on and begin again. I named all these ghosts after all the things we've done together. At the same time, I named them after your changes, after your sudden loss of interest, in your sudden loss of excitement to see me. I named them after your forgotten promises. I named all these ghosts after everything that we've been through and how it ended up being just me without you. I named this pain after you — my favorite painful ghost I could no longer invite to sleep with me.

DARK THOUGHTS

It is just another day of not knowing what to do with my thoughts. It's just another day of breaking myself again from overthinking too much. The past — they always creep in. They always remind me why I don't deserve to be happy, why I have to be completely stranded in the haunting past that I could no longer change.

It's eating me up alive. It's breaking me so bad that it deletes the memory of how I used to love myself. All I see is a person with crocheted mistakes on her skin. I grew so distant from people and even from myself. I was skilled when it comes to breaking my self-esteem. All my motivation was drowned in oblivion that I didn't know how to begin once more. I was constantly lost for years now without knowing where to go. Everyone wants me out. Everyone's too hateful.

I know that it is my responsibility to make myself happy but how can I? How can I be that happy when everything that I do always leads to another fatal error that I could no longer undo? How can I believe in chances when all that ever see is judgment and a standoffish circle of high-end people?

How can I be happy when the world never ran out of ways to remind me why I should stay mad and sad for not being the person I wished to be.

KEPT SADNESS

I was afraid to tell everyone about my sadness. I know most of them will never understand. I started hiding it since I was young. All my negative views about life, I either write it or just pretended that I already forgot about it. But the more I stop myself from feeling that sadness, the more it makes me want to explode.

I don't want to share it, for I knew that sadness is contagious, and I don't want others to feel blue as well. I don't want them to hate me for giving them some of my storms, for adding black on their photos, for being the reason why they stopped seeing the good in life. So I stop myself from sharing the details of why I feel sad out of nowhere, why I became silent when they're in the middle of cracking their jokes. I grew so used to stopping myself from dropping some of the skeletons of my loneliness for it will leave them the stains of my wretchedness.

I am so used to feeling all of this all at once
—all alone. And I don't know if this is my way of
saving myself or breaking. All I know is I want to
save them from me.

ONLY THING LEFT

People always leave me like it's the fastest and easiest way to do it. They break what they can break and never ask for an apology. I would sit there in one corner asking myself why people always hurt me when they get the chance to do so. And so I keep their voices inside my pocket. I carry it everywhere I go until I would collapse and start crying in the middle of a crowd. I would cry and cry and cry, and my heart will tighten up, but I still don't have the words to explain where the pain truly came from.

I don't know how I should name this pain. My depression makes me want to prison myself out from everyone until I end up blending on the jet-black walls and listen to the conversations that my monsters wanted to build up. I would stare and pretend I am half dead. I want to unload my life from this void that resided within me. I want to just stop feeling everything, I don't care if I won't be happy anymore as long as I don't get this sad.

I want to stop the pain but what if it's the only thing that's left for me to feel?

IS THIS KARMA?

Is this karma? Is this the thing that I will get for leaving someone who loves me to pursue someone who doesn't love me? Is this the thing that I will get for closing my doors for the love that's been offered to me with sincerity? Do I deserve this rejection because I rejected people who did nothing bad to me? Was it really meant for me to watch someone tell me I was out of his league just because I told others I don't want their persistence?

I think about this all the time —times I was so viciously forbidding to people who only had good intentions to me. I was completely ashamed of how I rip their hearts with my honesty and hushed them all before I could get to hear their points. I was so occupied with the reverberations of their pleadings, it started to conquer my thoughts. I didn't know that I will also be in their shoes. I never knew this pain would hurt more than words could say. I was completely unconscious of how bad I was for not explaining to them why I can't love them. All I gave were shrill words and loud sounds of shutting doors.

Is this the pain that I deserve to receive for breaking so many hearts before? is this the pain I deserve to receive just because I love so true?

SADDER DAYS

The nights were a little darker and longer, the city outside was still in the highest peak of energy it could ever have. Everyone's out there enjoying the lights, the stars, the company, and good old friends. Everyone's out there unfolding the different definitions of being alive. Everyone's out there, breaking rules, climbing on fences, kissing strangers, drinking booze until they pass out, and creating memories they will endlessly call a good flashback.

Everyone's out there, all-out happy without being terrified of what will happen next. They take in every second with new-found experiences, capture every moment that spell out life. They all showed up with happy faces, they all showed up extent bliss. Everyone out there lived their life to the fullest I wonder if they're familiar with loneliness. I wonder if some of them get to go home into empty hallways and distant love from family. I wonder if some of them are truly happy when it's just them alone the same way they were if they're under the blinding lights of the clubs.

All I know is that most of them are out there because they wanted to be distracted or to be happy. It was a way to escape the chaos life never gets tired of giving. And here I am, locked inside the room with heavy curtains and turned-off lights. The nights were a little darker and longer, I never knew I could be sadder than this.

GOOD REVENGE

When I was young, I thought the greatest karma that I could give to people who hurt me is to make them feel the exact dense of sadness that they gave me. I thought hurting them back would make me feel better. I thought I could get the satisfaction of watching them suffer, of being in pain.

But later on, I realized that the greatest karma that I could give to them is my success, my happiness, and my willingness to keep going despite how much they wanted to stop me from moving forward on my own. I realized my happiness is something that they don't want to witness, that my victory is something that they don't want to hear. So I will work on it. I will motivate myself to continue walking, to continue searching for a reason why I should be better than what they expected me to be. I will be better; I will not do it just for them. I will do it for myself. I will give them the bad karma that they never likely to have.

I will smile more often. I will dance more freely. I will write more courageously. I will be alive. I will be happy. I will annoy them with my happiness.

IT'S ALL UP TO THE WORLD

You have no idea how damaged I was the same day you decided to leave everything behind like what we started meant nothing to you. You have no idea how it broke me into shreds that I didn't know how to begin once again. Somehow, you took everything you could. You brought everything well-packed in a raft you called your sacred emotions. You wanted to pull out everything you could reach even if it means it has to leave me so hopelessly empty with no traces of hope. For the longest time, I allowed you to invade my soul, to tell me what I should do. I allowed you to turn my dreams into a condensation that's too invalid for me to share with anyone.

You wanted to use me to fill in the lapses of your inconsistency, to clean the shards of the beer bottles you broke every night. You wanted someone to be there, to follow up on your mess, and to have a punching bag for your inconsiderate behaviors. And as you finally left me too decoyed on the floor, I wished you'll just get a taste of your

own poison. I get to wished you'll end up hurt —
double the pain that you gave me.

I hope you'll get to feel the exact pain that
you gave me. I hope this time, the world will come
in my favor.

BE CAUTIOUS

Always be cautious about how you treat people. Always be observant about other people's level of sensitivity, watch the words you use. Be careful how it would affect them. Always think before you do something bold, always check the ripples if it bounces back. Always think before you put something into action. Always be careful with actions for life holds karma. We get good karma if we do good things. We get bad karma if we do the opposite. And that's why it's a little something if we try to do things with consciousness. It's a good thing that we get to experience a little fright if we take a decision. It's something that separates us from commenting on a completely wrong move. The fear of bad karma makes people more attached to aiming to maintain a good conscience, so we do good things in high hopes of receiving a rewarding feeling in return.

Anyhow, that's the real reason why I wanted to be vigilant. I need to be thoughtful not to hurt people through my unfiltered words. I want to make up for the promises that I made. I want to erase the probabilities of spitting out lies, to watch people break because of my inept engagements. I just want to live life with a fear of what's to come. It makes me want to be a good person in this world filled with cruel people.

IN HOPE OF THE WORLD WITH ETHICS

Please don't leave me here. This world only lives in black and grey. They see what's right clear and loud, but they always side with the wrong. They see resolutions, answers to the problems, but they take insidiously the places reserved for them with abusive powers nobody could control.

Please don't leave me here. The city I live in holds so much superiority. They control the people and they break the rules. They refuse to live up to their words. They refuse to relive the code of ethics they articulated. It's a place filled with many obnoxious hands slipping under the drawers of people's hope — constantly stealing what people know nothing about.

Please don't leave me here. This place is stuffed with people who go with the vile and leave the ones who want to change the world for the better. They want to silence the truth and hush the voices who wanted to speak on behalf of them.

I am so sick of living in this unethical world. I am sick of waking up every morning and see how people refuse to burn bridges between good and evil. I am tired of settling down to what's here. I just want to see what the world would be like if we did things ethically — together.

SEPARATED

We got used to this — living at the same time yet with different perceptions and perspectives toward seeing and understanding things.

We were all separated by race, how our skin color stood like the only façade that matters most to people's first impressions. The colorism started to divide unity like continents with restricted borders to unwelcome exiles.

We are all separated by gender, always using this-and-that arguments. We refused to emphasize, to see what's beyond the decisions. We neglect the chances to see what's beyond the reasons as we failed to open our hearts towards to love everyone. We limit our circle and stay out from those we can't accept.

We are all separated by religion, always demand the majority to follow one's beliefs. We loathe those who go in contrast; we hate the ones we can't change. We wanted to shove to them what we believe in and cross them out when they refuse to do it.

We are all separated by reasons, by views, by small or big whys and wherefores. We wanted to be right by highlighting the ones that don't satisfy you, without seeing your words cut like a knife. We wanted to be the right people — yet we refused to be good and ethical.

CHANGE

I was always asked to change.

As I look at myself through the mirror, I don't actually know where or how to begin changing myself. All I see is a body that needs acceptance. I see vulnerability and weak bones that fear the creeks of the nights when I am walking alone in the dark alley. I was asked to dress nicely, to stop showing too much skin. I was asked to wear longer skirts, to stop wearing shorts, to walk with modesty, to attract people I want to settle with.

I see no reason why I have to change. All I see is a body that aims to bloom during the day and night. All I see is a person who has nothing but just the wish to be respected without, restricting myself from feeling everything that would make me personally happy.

I see a body that has imperfect curves, with a crooked-teeth smile, uneven skin and a burned-out heart and all I ever wished to be is to live in a world with words that don't always break someone's confidence. I want to be surrounded by people who know how to filter inappropriate opinions before speaking up. I want to live in a changing environment where everyone is welcome to bloom with grace.

RIGHT THINGS

Always choose to do the right things.

Always help when you get the chance, with or without witnesses. Always help without needing for the world to see it. Always offer a shoulder to cry on for someone whose world is slowly crumbling down. Be the reason why they want to give life another shot of chance.

Always choose to stay kind, to be openhearted toward listening. Always bring on the right words and heal a breaking heart with it. Always choose to be the one who stays brave, who stays honest and assured. Always keep up with the promises you made and the one who brings contagious happiness.

Always choose to be the person who manages to correct someone's wrongs and to guide them until they're finally back on track. Always choose to be the one they could run to when the world turns a little nasty and disturbing. Be their hope; be their sample of courageousness. Be their healing, their happiness, and their optimism.

Always choose to be the person who lives in peace, the person who wanted to believe that this world is not that bad at all. Always choose to do things right, for it's easier to explain than mistakes.

Be remembered for your goodness.

SOMETHING

I know there's something that I need to know, And I really don't know how to name it. I could sense them in your sudden changes, in your sudden disinterest in the things that used to bring you the highest heights of happiness. I sensed it in your loss of focus or reserved time after work to get it to spend with me.

I sensed that there's more to your changes, and it's not just the changes that only take one week or one month. I knew it was kind of different, for you started to sound like a stranger to me. Your discomfort makes me feel uncomfortable. Your sudden short-tempered approach made me want to keep my excitements aside and give you silence hoping it will save you and give you peace of mind. Your I-love-yous were too dry, your hand holding mine felt so loose. I knew it was the kind of change that I don't need to ask you why it has to happen. My intuition answered it all. My instinct has always been right. It was always brutally honest.

I watched you change every single day. I watched my heart break every single day too. I knew my intuition never lies. Tell me you're falling out of love with me.

ONE'S MIND

Never think of keeping other people's voices inside your head just because they wanted to turn you into someone they want. Free your mind with their toxicity. Your mind is not a rental room that lets people come in and break everything they could before they leave just because they knew it was not them who own them. People wanted to invade empty spaces and fill them with so much contagion. They want to manipulate, to poison your thoughts until you start seeing the world through the wrong lenses. They will tell you what to become without asking you what you wanted for yourself.

So make sure that your mind is a place where people's toxic words can't get in. Never allow them to trespass. Never allow them to tell you to keep it open 24/7. Never give them the free pass or the keys. Make negative people feel like they are your unwanted guests, so their actions will turn a little stiff until their words would start shame themselves when spoken.

Have your own say. Be your own hero. Be your own listener and speaker. Just be your own voice.

DECISIONS

Here's the thing about intuition — it gives me a perfect shortcut to make these rapid verdicts. It doesn't make me want to cling to a single idea for a long time until it eats my sanity away, but there's a little fear of not picking the correct decision between the two.

A part of me was a little afraid that it would only mislead me into the dark corners of the world with locked doors and no hope for a way out. I was afraid to hear only the echoes and not the real sound of decisions; but despite that, I still trust the other half of me that speaks about what I should do. I will slowly unleash fear, I will slowly set aside doubts.

I know my intuition is taking me somewhere, and I am ready to get lost along with it until I find the real meaning of my existence.

MY INTUITION

They always say I should trust my intuition for it never lies. They said I should follow what my heart wanted me to do, that I should never delimit from crossing boundaries if the answers were seen across. Somehow, it's the battle between knowing about the cruel truth or getting along with comfort when it comes to the comfort of the lies. Maybe that was the reason why I stayed in the mediocre, of always wanting to give myself a little hold back towards running after what my intuition is telling me. I am in hesitation towards trusting the strength of my heart — of how extent it could carry the heaviness of the cruel truth.

My intuition never lets me sleep peacefully at night. It leaves a resonating sound that never stopped reminding me about the dark secrets that are peaking on my heavy curtains, about the heard footsteps of the lies I kept with the house. It never lets me find peace for it always screams for me to know. it's waiting for me to pursue it, to unleash it

— to free it even it means it has to break every single bone that I have in me.

So maybe my intuition never lies, it's just that I am not yet ready to get hurt.

BE CRUEL AS YOU

I wish I could hurt you so badly that you'll spend years healing the scars I left in your skin. I wish I could hurt you with words until it rips our soul apart from the same way you hurt me, the same way you broke the core of me.

I wish I could use the same lies that you used on me, so you'll get to have a deal of your own paranoia when the world suddenly went sound asleep. I want you to stay wide awake wondering what's wrong with you the same way I asked myself what's missing in me that you never felt so contented with my being.

I wish I could hurt you so disdainfully bad that you'll start wondering when you will begin healing yourself, which part of your body you should change first the same way you filled me with reasons to be insecure about my appearance. I want you to feel like you're running out of reasons to be happy, too drained you'll begin hating other people's happiness too.

I want to break you, but I know I can't. I could never turn myself into a monster like you. I could never do that, so I'll leave everything to karma.

LOVE KNOWS NO GENDER

She loves her. It's more than just a pronoun or another typo error that must be corrected. It was something that they felt real and at the same time, they felt right to feel.

She loves her and that goes with no explanation. She realized she was her sunrise, the reason for her to see the goodness of beginnings. She was the reason why she learned to appreciate herself, to understand the ways on how to value her feelings. Somehow, we grew in a society that dictates that women are for men and men are for women empowered by the verses on the bible, but she was up for something different. She knew what her heart was telling her. She knew that there's nothing wrong in chasing the love that has done nothing wrong.

To fall in love with the right person is equivalent to making one person feel that she has also fallen into the right place where her self-worth is not threatened. She realized it a long time ago and that she found the luxury of precious moments in her. She was her great love — the reason why she learned to trust again.

Love knows no gender. It only knows the comfort of home.

WHY SHE LOVES HER

It all started with simple conversations — sharing of interests, sharing of favorite songs, and timeless films. It all began on the surface until time permitted them to share something about life. She was the talker and the other 'her' was the listener. They shared so much about almost everything, how every topic enthralled them. She started hearing her brave tales while the other one found the courage to speak about something she haven't shared with anyone else. The trust was established; the comfort was welcoming. It was impossible not to fall for someone whom you had the chance to have a glimpse of her most sacred side that nobody else has ever seen — her wandering soul, her wonderful mind, and her forgiving heart.

She fell with her softness, her sudden outburst of laughter. She fell in love with her genuineness, with how she viewed things, how she fought back against all the adversities that she was forced to face. She fell for her day after day.

That's when she knew she couldn't live without her. She realized that love was not just affection or physical attraction. She fell for her because she was being herself. She loved her and that was it. It's something worth fighting for.

CLOSET

It took me years and within those years, I hid inside the closet where nobody would come to see even just an edge of my true color. Not being straight was too costly to share, and it's like acceptance was something I couldn't buy. I was scared to step even just a single toe outside. I was craving for someone who would tell me that it's okay to be myself, that there's nothing wrong with being who I truly was. I was craving for someone who would embrace me although my colors were too bright that it blinded those who had remorse for it.

It was so easy to pretend to be someone you're not, but why was it too risky to tell the world the real you? I was so confused that I ended up hating myself for not being just like anyone else. I grew so tired of explaining my true self because everything that I received in return was shrill stares and confusion that would only make everything worse.

I am still here, still caged inside my own closet, surrounded by infinite darkness that I named after my terrors, my seclusion, my beating secrets. I want to get out, but the crowd outside scares me the most.

WHAT THEY DON'T KNOW

It's still a cruel world out there. Still filled with stares that antagonize the soul — mean enough to damage it. That's the reason why I was too afraid to tell them about you — because most of them wouldn't understand why a woman has to fall to another woman when there were lots of other fish in the sea. They didn't understand what they didn't already know because they closed their minds towards seeing the possibility of how and why it all happened naturally. Sadly, they would always give us the look of disgust when I sat next to you closer, when I was about to hold your hand, or even just looked at you straight in the eye. They would give us the clearest disapproval when we learned to muster up the courage of telling them we're willing to give them reasons.

Somehow, they would never know how you stayed with me when I was dealing with my own storms they would never know how your words healed me, how your laughter calmed me. They would never know how you brought out the best of me when I felt like I was in my worst state. They would never understand something they didn't know. What they don't know — they can't breakaway.

DEAR GOD

It's been a long time since I last talked to you because somehow, I stopped believing in you. I stopped believing that you exist because every prayer that I cried myself to sleep with was ignored. It feels like you never listened to my pleadings. You never listened to my begging. You never listened to the times I cried for help.

I felt so alone and stoped believing that you were real. It was the darkest days of my life, and it felt like I was wasting my time calling the name who was never proven to exist. I stoped believing in other's toxic positivity, claiming I should rely on you when I felt like I should stop trusting my colleagues. They said you might not be heard but you listen to every prayer. How was that even possible? There were so many people who were praying different prayers all at the same time. How was is even possible that my outcry would be heard? I stopped holding onto my faith and stopped talking to you. Years have come and gone, and I am still an unbeliever.

I still refused to open my heart. I don't know if you truly exist, or were you just being a little unfair?

IN THE MIDDLE

They said I should believe in God, I should believe in His supremacy, I should hold onto my fate for it will one day that would save me. I don't believe in heaven nor in hell. I don't believe I am going anywhere either of the two. I don't believe in the paradise they poisoned in my head when I was a kid where there'll be a waiting place where there's no pain, a paradise filled with wonderful colors that would simmer down all the stings of heartache that you felt when you were alive. I also grew up hearing that bad people fall into hell where no part of our skin will be left unburned. It was so easy to manipulate the innocent minds of the kid and make them believe in heaven and hell, that there are God and Satan.

It was also their way of defining morality, to provide a profound example that would make everything easier to explain or picture out.

Hence, just as much as I want to believe, there's still a science that captivates my heart. There are people who work on the numbers, patterns, theories that would give me more solid proof why we're here.

I don't know how everything works, which among these contrasts weighs more.

I just want to be on the mediocre.

COMICAL

Gather together; wear cream clothes as the bonfire blazes. The night is silent, but the birds were chirping like investigators looking for receipts to burn them down. They take the stars as chandeliers, soon witnessing how they chant lost-in-rhyme prayers, calling the names of their false prophets and gods. They claim the end of the world and how they will be the only people left to be saved. They pray as they cry; they cry as they pray. They were possessed by insanity, holding onto the faith they never knew where it truly came from. They believed the verses handwritten by a person, no testimony of its existence. One person leads, while the other one follows. They started looking like fools baptized by empty promises of the afterlife. They scream names, they follow like pets.

They hurdle the reality by the subsequent quest of wanting to be saved in the future.

The night stood still, the chants were louder —passionate. They believe what they think would mend their souls and prevented themselves to see reality in the modern age of the world. It's both a blessing and a curse to believe in something peculiar.

DIVISION

An atheist —not good, not bad just like anyone else. Always perceived as the antagonist in the eyes of faith-believers. Always met with a microscopic stare from head to toes, scrutinizing every corner of their being as a temple with a hidden weakness that will soon collapse.

They never stepped into the church, refused to correlate hopes with prayers. They refused to call a name they hadn't met, not seen even just a trace of his face. They refuse to open their hearts to believe what lack studies, and some church-goers fail to see them as anyone else. The partition that splits two differences became more like a fault line that has the unseen depth, nobody dares to cross the line. Nobody dares to listen to one side.

Atheists preferred to rely upon their perception of life and faith in what has been explored in the past years. They wanted to invest their fate to what has been proven to be true, to what has undergone prolonged research.

This division will linger; it will stay, and it will continue to divide everybody.

The separation that nobody else could bind again.

ALL THE PEOPLE I HATE WERE THERE

I remember when I was twelve, I went to church. I was on my favorite flowery pastel dress mom bought at a cheap boutique. I would wear my usual white glossy shoes with lacy socks. Mom would braid my hair into halves. I would watch her fix her formal clothes, pat a powder on her cheeks, put a little lipstick on her lips, and would constantly check her watch every single moment she could get.

As we reached the church, she would meet people along the way. The woman who greeted her on the doorstep was a well-known mistress who took another woman's husband and disregarded the abandoned children. I would sense mom wanting to end the conversation as soon as she can. There's also a man that would sit in front of our pew, famous enough to be a child molester but no hint on his tuxedo suit, and perfectly gelled hair.

The priest will soon start the mass, gradually proceeding to the homily then throwing ad hominem to unnamed people, speaking about goodness while spilling ugly words that are too corrupting to younger people like me.

They said the church is filled with people who believe in God, the self-proclaimed righteous ones. I hated it. It was by then, I started hating going to church – a solemn place where a crowd of evil people gather calling themselves angels.

Isang Tasa ng Tsaa Para Sa'yo

"Sa pinakamadilim na sandali ng
ating buhay, kailangan nating magtuon
upang makita ang liwanag."
—Aristotle

***

Ang mga akda sa kabanatang ito ay kuha sa mga piling *journal* at *literary notebook* na naisulat ng manunulat noong nasa ika-pito hanggang ika-siyam na gulang pa lamang ito at noo'y nasa antas tersyarya. Sa panahon ding iyon siya nagsimulang magsanay sumulat ng iba't ibang akdang pampanitikan sa wikang Filipino at Ingles. Upang mapanatili ang noong diskarte at istilo sa pagsulat ng may akda. Hiniling nito na huwag galawin, baguhin o palitan ang ano mang bahagi ng orihinal niyang piyesa. Samakatuwid, ang mga piling tula at prosa na inyong mababasa ay hango mismo sa orihinal na katha at nailimbag na hindi dumaan sa masusing pagsusuri.

PILOTO

Ako ay isang piloto
Mataas ang nililipad
Mapa umaga man o gabi
Ako ay naglalayag

Masilayan ang araw
Hanggang ang dilim ay lumiwanag
Paglubog ng araw
Hanggang sa huling sinag na maaaninag

Nakakapagod na
Nakakulong sa himpapawid
Iba't ibang lugar ang tinatawid
Minsan naiiwan sa pagitan ng dilim at liwanag

Nang di ko nababatid
Nakatulala sa malayo
Parang gusto nang ihatid
Sarili sa pinakamadilim na sulok
Lugar kung saan alam lahat ng lihim at sikreto
Lulutang sa kalawakan
Ligtas sa mga mata ng bagyo at delubyo

Kaisa ng mga tinitingalang bituin

Na alam aking mga hilig
Ngunit nakakulong sa loob ng isang eroplano
Sa isang madilim at masikip na kwarto
Ano mang hiling na ibagsak
Aking sinasakyan
Hindi ako magkaroon ng tapang
Maski makayanan...

MULI

Alas otso na! Gigising na! Tatanghaliin ka na sa paborito mong palabas sa telebisyon!

Mamadaliing bumangon upang makakain at mailipat sa paboritong istasyon. Habang nanonood ay pinapangarap mong isa ka sa mga Superhero na malalakas at lumalaban sa mga masasamang kampon. Pagkatapos manood kagyat ng lalabas ng bahay upang tawagin ang mga kalaro at mag-unahan ng makahanap ng pato. Maglalaro na ng piko, manghihingi na ng lata at patibayan na ng tsinelas sa tumbang preso, magpapagalingan na ng pagpapaikot kapag nagsimula ng maglabasan ng trumpo, magsisilabasan na rin ang mga magagaling umiwas sa patintero. At ang mahuli naman sa taya-tayaan ay mapupugo.

Pagkauwi'y, kakain ng tanghalian at maya-maya pa'y iidlip na upang mag siesta. Ang pagiging bata ay nakakamiss din talaga. Noong dekada nobenta maski payak ay masaya. Hindi alintana ang pagod at problema. Ngunit ngayon, Hindi na natin nagagawa ang dating nakagawian. Pati pato iaalay para lang sa mga bagay na walang kasiguraduhan, hindi na pwede maging lata para lamang patumbahin, makikipagsapalaran sa tunay na buhay at susunod sa ikot ng mundo, iiwasang magkamali upang sa dulo ay hindi mahuli.

At muli, sa aking pagkakahimbing nawa'y manumbalik ang nakaraan. Mga nakaraang pilit nating nililingon, ngunit hindi na maaaring balikan. Mga ala-alang kinapulutan ng maraming-aral sa buhay at mga taong minsa'y naging parte ng ating pagbabago.

Ngunit..... Nasaan na nga ba sila?

Nasaan na ang mga naglalarong bata?

AKAY 'TAY

Ako ang bunso sa magkakapatid at nag-iisang gwapo sa aming apat. Hindi ako normal kung iyong nababatid. Ang hilig ko ay makipaglaro ng bahay-bahayan. Ako ang magulang ngunit nanay-nanayan. Kahit na hinuhulmang maton, hindi ko pa rin maiwasan ang maglaro ng baton. Labing pulang-pula, dahil sa kending krayola. Aking tinatakpan mga pasa ng pekeng pamada. Magmukhang maganda upang maging katanggap-tanggap sa karamihan. Umay na sa pamumuna at panlalait. Mula sa aking amang ako ay itinatakwil. Dahil ang aking pagkalalaki ay hindi ko raw na-feel. Ang chaka na lagi akong pinapalayas. Di alam kung saan boborlog kapag ako'y tumatakas. Araw-araw na jombag ang aking inaabot. Ang balat ko na sa hanash ay kumukulubot. Iyak dito, iyak doon hanggang lungkot ay mapawi.

Ngunit kahit anong tiktak talak ng tatay. Handa akong ma-chugi, sa aking Pudrang iaalay. Hindi ko ipagpapalit ang galit sa bait. Salamat pa rin ako'y iyong hindi ipinagpalit. Alam kong wala kang magagawa kung ako'y shokla. Pero nandito lang ako sa tabi mo hanggang pagtanda. Akay-akay ka sa bawat problema sa mundo. Magkasakit ka ma'y, ako ang mag-aalaga sa iyo. Hindi sa pagiging bading nababase ang kagandahang-asal, kundi sa puso. Nasa puso ang bait. Hindi maluluwa kahit pa masakal. Lahat ng pait aking lulunukin. Basta ang aking itay balang araw, ako'y tanggapin.

HULING HAPUNAN

Umaga pa lamang ibinando nang lumikas ang mga tao, maraming nag-alangan dahil mukha namang walang magyayari, maaliwalas ang kalangitan, tahimik ang kapaligiran. Sa kabilang banda ay marami na ring pamilya ang nagdesisyon na lumikas na, ang iba ay nagtataas na ng mga gamit na posibleng abutin ng baha. Sa isang sulok nag-iisip ang isang bata, iniisip niya na kumbinsihin ang mga magulang na lumikas at maghanda ng mga pagkain, tubig, mga gamot dahil iyon ang itinuturo sa paaralan, ngunit wala silang pera at sapat lamang sa maghapong pagkain ang kinikita ng magulang nito kaya imposibleng may maiimbak sila.

May mga bagay nga talaga na hindi inaasahang mangyari, nang mag hapon ay nagsimula nang umulan ng malakas, bawat patak nito ay lumilikha ng ingay sa yerong bubong, ang hangin ay tila sumisipol sabay sa pag-wagayway ng mga puno sa labas. Padilim na ng padilim, habang nasa hapag-kainan ay masaya silang nag-uusap na parang ito na ang huli. Tila ba'y hindi inda kung anuman ang posibleng mangyari. Patulog na ang mag-anak na parang normal na gabi lang ang mayroon sila, hanggang sa kalagitnaan ng gabi, napakadilim at tanging gasera lamang ang ilaw.

Palakas ng palakas ang hangin na nakakapagpauga na sa kanilang bahay na gawa lamang sa kahoy at yero, umiingay na rin ang yero na wari'y matatanggal sa lakas ng hangin. Lumakas lalo ang buhos ng ulan na tila ba'y ibinubuhos nito ang galit ng kalikasan.

Tumaas na ang tubig na kanina'y wala naman. Wala pang isang oras ay pataas na ng pataas ito na umaabot na hanggang bewang. Hindi nag-panic ang mag-asawa dahil mayroon silang bangka, nag-gayak na sila upang magtungo sa malapit na evacuation center, at sinigurong maayos na naisara ang kanilang tahanan bago umalis.

Habang namamangka ang padre de pamilya, ang kanyang mag-ina ay siyang nag-tatanggal ng tubig sa loob ng bangka dulot ng malakas pa ring pag-ulan. Patuloy itong nag sagwan hanggang sa rumagasa ang malakas na agos ng tubig na syang naging dahilan upang tumaob ang sinasakyan nilang bangka. Madali silang nag ayos at sumakay muli. May narinig silang sigaw na di kalayuan sa kinaroroonan nila kaya hinanap nila ito.

Habang binabagtas nila ang kinaroroonan ng sigaw ay maraming kumakapit sa bangka at humihingi ng tulong at nagpupumilit makisakay. Sinasabi nila na maghanap muna ng mataas na lugar pansamantala, at babalik sila upang ilikas ang iba. Ngunit sadyang mapilit ang mga ito. Marami na ang umiiyak dahil sa pagod kalalangoy. Paulit-ulit na sinabi ng mag asawa na babalik silang muli at sa pagkakataong iyo'y may kasama na silang tanod na tutulong, ngunit parang walang narinig ang mga ito, patuloy lamang sapag akyat, itunutulak na sila ng sagwan ngunit patuloy silang kumakapit, hanggang sa rumagasa ang napakalakas na agos ng tubig dahilan upang tumaob muli ang sinasakyang bangka ng mag-anak. Puro tulong at iyak ang maririnig sa kalagitnaan ng gabi.

Ang pamilya na sana'y magiging daan upang makahingi ng tulong, ngayo'y nangangailangan na rin ng tulong. Sigaw sila ng sigaw ngunit tila bingi ang sinumang makarinig, pinipilit nilang lumangoy upang makahinga sa ibabaw ng napakalalim na tubig. Habang nakalubog sa tubig. Ang bata na kanina'y nasa sulok, nasabi nito sa kanyang isip...

"Sana pala'y pinilit ko ang nanay at tatay na lumikas, sana niyakap ko sila ng mahipit at nasabing mahal na mahal ko sila, sana pala..."

Hanggang sa nilamon na siya ng alon at tuluyan nang pumikit...

'NAY, NARITO NA ANG PANSIT!

Maagang nagising si Alvin ngayong araw. Maliban kasi sa may trabaho ito, ngayon din ang araw ng pasahod ng kanilang kumpanya. Kaya naman masaya ang gising niya at ganadong-ganado pumasok. Bago siya pumasok ay inasikaso na muna niya ang inang may sakit. Dinalhan niya ito ng almusal sa kwarto at kinwentuhan.

"'Nay, hayaan niyo pag nakaluwag-luwag ako dadalhin kita sa ospital upang magamot na ang iniinda nyong karamdaman." Sabi niya habang hinahaplos-haplos ang ulo nito.

"Huwag mo na akong intindihin anak, matanda na ako at bilang na rin ang nalalabi kong araw sa mundo. Isipin mo ang kinabukasan mo. Gawin mo lahat ng gusto mong gawin habang bata ka pa. Para wala kang pagsisihan sa huli." Wika nito ng may pangangaral.

"'Nay naman, huwag po kayong magsalita ng ganyan. Mabubuhay pa po kayo ng matagal.

Gagawin ko ang lahat upang humaba pa inyong buhay. Hindi ko po kakayanin ang buhay ng wala kayo sa tabi ko. Kayo lang po ang dahilan ng aking pagsusumikap. Kaya naman ang pakiusap ko sa inyo ay lumaban kayo. Mahal na mahal kita 'nay. " wika nito habang yakap-yakap ang ina.

"Sige na, pumasok ka na sa trabaho. Ayos lang ako, magbihis ka na. Mag-iingat ka lagi. Kumain ka sa tamang oras." Inuubong sabi ng matanda.

"Opo 'nay. Siya nga po pala, bibilhan ko kayo ng gamot niyo mamaya pag-uwi. Ngayon po kasi bigayan ng sahod namin. Dadalhan ko rin po kayo ng paborito niyong pansit. Kaya naman hintayin niyo ako mamaya, sabay tayo kakain ng pansit ha. " nakangiting sabi nito sa ina.

Umalis na si Alvin ng bahay ng may maaliwalas na mukha at pumasok na nga ito sa kumpanya na kanyang pinagta-trabahuhan. Ngunit habang papasok ito, tila mayroon siyang napansin na kahina-hinala. Kaya naman binagalan nito ang kanyang lakad. Nang malapit na siya sa may pintuan ng kanilang opisina ay tumambad sa kaniya ang mga naglalakihang lobo at maraming pagkain.

"Congratulations Alvin!" sigaw ng mga katrabaho nito sa opisina.

Nang oras na iyon ay gulat na gulat siya at tila walang alam sa mga nangyayari. Kaya naman salitang "Salamat" na lamang ang kanyang nasabi. At dali-daling pinuntahan ang kanyang bisor upang magtanong. Ngunit sa pinto pa lamang ng Supervisor's Office ay nakita na niya ang boss niya na kumakaway at inaaya siyang pumasok.

"Congratulations Alvin! You did a great job. Ikaw ang napili ko upang pumalit sa posisyon ni Mr. Nico sa company. Since nalipat siya ng ibang Department. Ikaw ang gusto kong ilagay at humawak sa iniwan niyang posisyon. Especially, alam kong need mo ito, for the medication of you Mom. Kaya I hope kahit papaano natulungan kita. Pwede ka nang mag-umpisa ng trabaho mo as Administrative Officer today. Again, Congratulations." wika ng bisor habang kinakamayan siya.

"Nakakahiya man po, pero thank you so much Sir. Gagawin ko po lahat ng makakaya ko. Hinding-hindi ko po kayo bibiguin." sabi niya habang pinipigilan nitong maluha.

Matapos ang buong araw niyang pagtatrabaho. Masaya itong lumabas ng kumpanya at dumaan sa malapit na ATM upang kumuha ng buwanang-sahod. Pagkatapos, dumaan na rin ito sa may malapit na butika upang bumili ng gamot ng kanyang ina.

Bago umuwi ay minabuti niya munang bumili ng mainit-init na pansit sa may kanto upang pagsaluhan nilang mag ina sa bahay. Nang makabili, dali-dali na itong naglakad pauwi. Ngunit laking pagtataka nito, nang marating niya ang iskinita papunta sa kanilang bahay ay may naaninagan siyang malalaki at maliliwanag na ilaw sa malayo. Noong una'y hinayaan niya lamang ito, at patuloy na naglakad, kalauna'y napagtanto niya na sa kanilang bahay pala nanggagaling ang ilaw na natatanaw niya sa may kalayuan.

Nang pasukin nito ang kanilang bahay, naabutan niyang umiiyak at nagdadalamhati sa may tapat ng puting kabaong ang malalapit nitong kamag-anak. Habang naririnig ni Alvin ang mga iyak at sigaw ng pagluluksa, kinabahan na ito at dali-daling hinanap ang ina. Nang makita niya itong nakahiga sa loob ng kabaong, dito na niya nabitawan ang hawak niyang pansit at humagulgol ng malakas habang niyayakap ang puting kabaong.

Nang gabing iyo'y gumuho lahat ng pangarap ni Alvin sa kanyang ina. Lalo na't kapo-promote lamang nito sa trabaho at pagkakataon na sana iyon upang maipagamot at maibigay ang mga pangangailangan nito.

Hindi pa rin mapigilan ni Alvin ang malungkot tuwing maaalala nito ang ina, kaya naman mas lalo pa niya pinaghusayan ang pagta-trabaho upang makamit lahat ng mga pina-pangarap niya. Nagsikap siya para sa sarili, at sa pinangako nito sa ina.

Ilang taon na rin ang lumipas mula nang pumanaw ang ina ni Alvin, ngunit hindi pa rin niya nalilimutan ang sakit buhat ng mamaalam ito. Sa ngayon, namumuhay na siya kasama ang kanyang mag-ina sa may exclusive subdivision malapit sa pinagta-trabahuhan nito. Madalas niya ring ikwento sa anak ang kabutihang loob ng kanyang ina noong nabubuhay pa ito.

Malayo na rin ang narating ni Alvin bilang isang Supervisor ng kanilang kumpanya. Lahat ng pangarap nito noon, ay kanya ng naisakatuparan.

Kaya naman tuwing araw ng kamatayan ng ina, hindi nawawala ang lutong pansit. Pansit na sana'y napagsaluhan nilang mag-ina bago ito sumakabilang buhay.

ALAS-DOSE

Sana ang mga kamay
Sa loob ng bilog ay magpantay
At hindi na muling maghiwalay
Ano mang unos at away
Pareho ang direksyong nilalakbay
Walang maiiwan bagkus ay sabay

Buong puso'y ibibigay
Hanggang sa dumating ang bukas
Saya ang matitirang bakas
Tuloy-tuloy sa pagkuha ng lakas
Sa isa't isa, hanggang makaalpas
Di alintana ang bilis ng oras

Sa ilang segundong tayo ay tutugma
Gagawin ang lahat upang hindi mawala
Dahil ito ang nakatakda
Nakasulat sa hangin at tadhana

Ang oras natin ay parang bula
Biglaang mawawala nang di inaakala

Kahit sa ilang segundo
Nagtagpo tayo sa gitna

Walang magpipilit gumitna
At walang mamamagitan
Sa sandaling hangganan
Sana alas-dose na lang muli
Upang mayakap ka't muling makatabi

PANGARAP

Huwag nating hayaan ang pangarap natin.
Ay maging pangarap na lamang habang buhay.

Bumangon tayo sa umaga.
Kumain at punuin ang sikmura ng bagong pag-asa.
Sapat man o kapos ang pahinga.
Gamitin ang buong araw.
Tungo sa ating pangarap.

Bumuo ng plano.
Gaano man kalupit at kalawak ang mundo.
Gumawa at maglista ng mga lugar.
Na gusto nating mapuntahan.
Gawin posible ang imposible.

Magtiwala sa ating sarili.
Mga kamay at paa na pagod na ngunit hindi
sumusuko.
Ang puso't isip na buo at kaya pang lumaban.

Sa ganitong pagkakataon.

Magtiwala tayo sa ating abilidad.
Magtiwala na balang araw lahat ng bagay.
Na ninanais natin ay magiging makatotohan.

LABAN

May mga laban ako sa buhay na mas minabuti kong takasan. Laban na alam kong sa huli ako ay talo. Mga laban na napaka imposibleng mapagtagumpayan. Sadya nga bang malupit ang tadhana sa akin? Baka naman ayaw ko lang, at ako mismo ang lumalayo sa mga bagay na nakatadhanang mangyari. Ngunit, Sulit nga ba lahat ng ipinaglaban ko? O lumaban lang ako sa wala? Sa bawat laban, ang pagkatalo nga ba ang batayan upang lumaban muli? O hudyat lamang ito upang tapusin kung ano mang ipinaglaban ko.

Kailangan nga bang takasan?

O bitawan?

Minabuti kong sumuko sa laban, upang matamo ang kapayapaan at kalayaan sa aking puso.

HANGGANG KAILAN?

Hanggang kailan mo kayang tiisin ang sakit? Mga sakit na ikaw lamang mismo ang nakakaalam at nakakaramdam. Hanggang kailan mo kayang itago ang luha? Mga luha na tanging unan mo lamang na basang-basa tuwing gabi ang saksi sa mga sakit na iyong nadarama. Hangang kailan mo kayang saktan ang sarili mo? Kailan mo pa kaya matatanggap sa sarili mo na hindi ka niya kilala at walang kayo? Hanggang kailan ka mag-iilusyon na kasintahan niya? Alam mo bang nasasaktan 'din ako sa tuwing nasasaktan ka.

Bawat pagtangis mo ay siya ring pag-agos ng aking mga luha. Kailan ka kaya makalalabas sa mundo na kung saan ay sinasabi mong ikaw ang bida at kayo ay magsing-irog. Ngunit hanggang kailan? Hanggang kailan ko kaya kayang hintayin matapos ang palabas sa telebisyon na pinamagatang Marimar? Para matapos na rin ang kahibangan niya na siya si Marimar at ako ang kasintahan niya at hindi si Sergio. Iba na talaga ang mundo ngayon, madalas pag-pantasyahan ang mga gwapo. Buti na lang ako si Angelika na handang ipakain ang kuwintas sa putik sa mga taong mang-aagaw at inggitera tulad ni Marimar.

The Voice within My Soul

"A soul that carries empathy. Is a
soul that has survived enormous pain"
—Carlos Medina

BURIED DEEP

Andrea and Sylvia have been best friends since 6th grade and now they are very much thankful that they are inseparable. They have faced many challenges especially in their senior year when Sylvia was cheated on by his two-year boyfriend, Andrea was there to comfort her. She even set Sylvia to random dates to ease the pain that her boyfriend caused her, but none of them was able to capture Sylvia's heart.

One time when Sylvia was bullied by some mean girls because she was a nerd. Now, Andrea and Sylvia are just laughing how Andrea was so courageous to fight those girls in front of the corridor. It was a scandal and Andrea was nearly expelled but she said that she only did that to protect her best friend.

Now they are going to college, and they are both sixteen, Andrea met this guy named Sixto who annoyed her so much yet after a year became her boyfriend in a year. Sylvia was very happy for Andrea and became friends with him.

It was a peaceful day at school and Andrea and Sixto were flirting in the locker when Sylvia came. It was time to go to their classes. Sixto planted a kiss to Andrea's lips and they bid goodbye to each other. Andrea walked with Sylvia to class, and you can literally see a huge smile from Andrea's face. She is totally smitten. While they were heading to class, Andrea cannot stop talking about Sixto and Sylvia just smiled awkwardly.

After class, Andrea was looking for her boyfriend because it seems that he was not answering her texts. Sylvia told her that his boyfriend might be busy with his class, but Andrea knew that his class was over an hour before she got out of her class. She showed the copy of Sixto's schedule. After half an hour of seeking her boyfriend, Andrea found out that her boyfriend was kissing another girl in the library.

Andrea was in rage, and she shouted in the library. She attacked both of them, and the librarian called the guards. Other students were looking at them. It was indeed a scandal. Andrea was crying, and she told Sixto and the girl hurtful words, but there's nothing that could ease the pain she was experiencing now. It's like the world has turned upside down, and her body was stabbed a million times.

Instead of apologizing to Andrea, Sixto told her that he was just looking for fun and definitely not ready for commitment. The situation was handled by the guards that came, and Andrea and Sylvia left in disappointment with a heavy feeling. Few weeks after Andrea was slowly recovering, she decided to never contact Sixto again and dispose any memories she had with him. But it is obvious that she suffered great pain for she lost weight, definitely cannot eat and sleep well.

One morning, Andrea did not feel well. She felt so tired and lazy waking up. In a few seconds, she immediately rushed into the comfort room and puked. Her head was dizzy and just a few snaps, she noticed that her period was delayed. She did not go to school that day. She did not tell her parents where she was going, and she bought a pregnancy test in a drug store.

The moment she went home she immediately tested and to her surprise, it was positive. It was not long when her parents knew about this and disinherited her. Her world was falling apart and all she could think of ending her life. She tried to tell the news to Sixto, but he refused to believe her.

For the time being, she was staying at Sylvia's house, but a few months passed she suffered from stillbirth and lost the baby. She was diagnosed with depression. Sylvia and her parents brought her to a Psychiatrist where she was treated which made her stop school.

But little did Sylvia and others know, Andrea was slowly giving up and never took her medicine. Due to severe depression, she was not eating and sleeping well. She grew thin and her heart could not handle the pain; she developed a heart disease which later on killed her.

A DISH BEST SERVED COLD

Prince Jude has always dreamt of having his own kingdom. For him, being the King meant that he could do everything and that he could always get what he wanted. He was chosen by his father King Douglas to be the heir of their kingdom, but in order for him to do that, he should find a woman to marry.

It's been months of preparation for the ball, so that Prince Jude could find the perfect woman for him. The ball was indeed spectacular, but Prince Jude couldn't find the one that he would love for the rest of his life but she needs to get married as soon as possible to inherit the position as a King.

Few months passed, Prince Jude has proven how worthy he was to be the next King. His father commended him, and the people loved him very much. Although he was a model to everyone, there was this duty and favor that he needed to fulfill which was to have a wife. It was his father's wish before he dies because he was already getting old. So, King Douglas arranged a marriage to their affiliated kingdom. Queen Sefira was his late wife's best friend and the wife of King Adam. It may be difficult for Prince Jude but he wanted to fulfill his father's wish, yet he also wanted someone whom he loved not just because they were arranged to get married.

At first, Prince Jude was not happy about his father's decision to the point that they argued about this. But then, they have scheduled a day to meet the affiliated kingdom. Queen Sefira and King Adam brought their daughter, Princess Camilla. She's an average looking Princess but you can see the humility in her eyes. She has long blonde hair and an average body. Not too thin and not too fat. She seemed kind and definitely gave him the impression that she was a responsible and smart woman.

During their lunch, both parties have exchanged random thoughts about politics, personal affiliations, and plans. It was in the middle of the conversation when the arranged marriage was brought up. Prince Jude and Princess Camilla made eye contact and it was not long when Prince Jude stood up, and excused himself.

That dinner was indeed nice, but both Prince Jude and Princess Camilla were not satisfied with the decision of their parents. One morning, they tried to get along with each other. They went horseback riding and visited some places in their land. It was fun, and from that day on, they became friends. They spent time together doing some stuff. They were together during kingdom meetings, appearances, events, and other personal events; eventually, they fell in love.

Both of their parents were very happy, but someone from a village came into King Douglas' kingdom, he sneaked out from the guards and was able to talk to the king. He claimed that his name was Erik and that the only son of Matilda who happened to be the first girlfriend of King Douglas. King Douglas loved her so much, but as the king, he had to leave her knowing she was pregnant.

The royal guard commanded the arrest of Erik for breaking in, but King Douglas stopped him. He gave Erik a chance to tell his story, so Erik showed the King a personalized necklace that the King gave to Matilda; with that he confirmed that he was his son. Everyone was so shocked, but King Douglas was thankful to meet his son.

Little did King Douglas know, Prince Jude was not happy to meet his half-brother. He argued with his father and told him not to believe the commoner but King Douglas was so determined that Erik was his. Erik told his father that the reason why he crashed the kingdom was because his mother was dying and they did not have any money for medication.

King Douglas agreed to help him and his mother who was once the love of his life. Slowly, King Jude developed anger toward his father and Erik. He became the rebel of the kingdom, and one night he planned to leave the kingdom and hide. He planned to ask Princess Camilla to go with him, but she refused because of her duties to her kingdom and her parents.

Prince Jude decided to walk away by himself. Years passed, and he has not lived a peaceful life. It was indeed difficult for him but he was so angry and envious on how his father treated his half-brother.

One day, he decided to return to the palace but to his surprise, he heard that Erik became the king and married Princess Camilla. King Douglas has passed away. He was so down and angry about the outcome, for he thought that his comeback would mean that everything would be okay again because he was ready to forgive and forget.

Upon knowing that, he threatened the kingdom and Prince Erik. He left the kingdom and gathered people who once believed in him. One night, they attacked the kingdom with their giant forks and torches. Guards halted, and the battle began. At last, the battle between the half brother happened, and King Erik was killed by his own half brother.

Jude laughed maniacally for he already killed the one who threatened him and brought him so much despair. He finally got his revenge, but Princess Camilla did not tolerate this kind of act; so she made Jude suffer the consequences by locking him up.

Jude finally got his revenge, but he was not free from severe sadness, wrath of others, and was locked up for his crime. Forever, it was embarked on his being that he killed his half brother and was dishonored Prince.

DON'T GIVE IN

John belonged to a very strict family; at a very young age, he always stayed indoors. He could still remember the times when he would just look at the kids playing outside through his window in his room. He had asthma that's why he's limited on most of his activities. Plus, he was the only child of his parents. But deep inside, he literally wanted to go out because he was tempted to make friends and to enjoy his youth.

Sometimes when he tried to ask his mother if he could go to his classmates' house for a review; he would always bring his nanny with him. His parents explained that it was to protect him, and they also told him that they could assure that whenever he would be having an asthma attack, his nanny would give him aid. He tried to sneak out a couple of times convinced by his classmates, but every time he does it, his conscience would bother him. So, he would just reject his emotions.

Years passed, and John got used to this set-up and even now that he is already 16 years old, his nanny would be there for him and if not, their family driver would drive him to school or somewhere. But he couldn't go to anywhere without his parents knowing. So, wherever he went the driver or himself should be inform his parents.

One time after class, his friends asked him if he could go to a party. Marcel was throwing a party because his parents would be out of town for weeks. He immediately grabbed his phone from his pocket about to call his parents when suddenly, his friends stopped him. Marcel told him that the party was safe and they assured that he would be protected because they have known John for years, and they wouldn't let anything happen to him.

Some of them even convinced John that it would not be necessary to call his parents if he truly trusted his friends. Marcel even joked around and said that John was already 16, and yet he had to consult his parents every time, so all of them laughed. They challenged John to go out of the house and told him that he was not defying his parents but showing them that he could do more now that he was all grown-up.

In the end, John refused to accept the offer of his friends and headed home. He was just quiet on the road. His nanny asked him what has been going on in his mind and told him nothing. He really wanted to go to that party. He was having second thoughts now. Is he going to the party meant that he was disobeying his parents or was it just one of the ways to enjoy life? Maybe going to the party didn't hurt if it was only just once.

Yes, sometimes he tried to stop himself from doing something he wanted, but there's this feeling in him that made him enjoy his living ever since. He felt the emptiness in him although he never disobeyed his parents. Looking at the ceiling while laying on his bed, he figured out that there was something missing. It's happiness.

That night, he called his friends and told him that he was going to the party. He sneaked out from his house and made it to the party. There, Marcel and his other friends welcomed him. It was indeed a loud party. People were dancing, some were making out and people were enjoying themselves.

Few moments later, when he was on his seat, Marcel got a tray of beer in his hands. He served it to his lads including John, but John refused to drink the alcohol because it might trigger his asthma; however, the alcohol and his friends were calling his name. Marcel and the others keep telling John that drinking is part of the party because one try couldn't kill you. Truly, they were tempting John to do something he has never done before.

It was like magnetism, and he immediately lifted the bottle. When he was about to take a sip, three girls approached them. Marcel kissed one of them. Others were happy because the other one was flirting with them. The other who sat beside John kept on flirting with him, but he was so awkward. The woman is caressing his chest and arms. He knew this was the end of him. He could feel that he wanted to give in and get this girl.

She was about to kiss him when he pushed her and told her to back off. The woman got upset and told him that he is a coward. Marcel asked why John did not give in. Marcel gave him a small plastic filled with small crystals; it was drugs. He told John to accept it as a thank you gift for attending his party. John stood up and said he was leaving. He did not even bid goodbye.

When he got home, he sneaked into his window, and when he made it in his room, he saw his parents looking at him. He apologized quickly, but his parents just hugged him. Her mother said, "See? We already told you that Marcel and his friends are just looking for fun and would definitely harm you." His dad agreed to what his mother said.

In the end, he was just thankful that his only defiance was sneaking out, and he did not give in to temptation of doing wrong and illegal things. From that day on, he truly understood his parents, and he was very grateful to have them.

WATCHING OVER YOU

Angelina was just a simple girl and the most humble person in their city. She has always been approachable. She had a good heart, so everybody loved her. Since she was young, she has always wanted to be a nurse so when she reached college, she took up nursing when she became a registered nurse, she truly made her parents proud.

Angelina never changed. She was packed with loads of responsibilities. As a nurse, her shift was not stable. Her shifts sometimes started at 11:00 p.m and ended at 8:00 a.m in the morning. Sometimes she would start at 1:00 p.m and end by 10:00 p.m. She got used to it in no time.

One time, when she was on a night shift, she saw a 7 year old boy in a hospital dress running and smiling. She looked at him and realized that it was her patient who had Leukemia. She noticed that he was being playful, she immediately told him not to play. The boy ran and went downstairs.

Angelina chased him and told him to go back to his room. She even asked why he was lurking when he should be staying in his room.

While she was chasing the boy, she happened to pass by his room, and there she realized that the doctor was already reviving him and his parents were crying. She was so shocked and already stopped chasing him. Her hands and feet felt cold. Her body felt entirely numb. A feeling that she couldn't describe.

Angelina thought that it would be the first and last time that she would experience that, but she was wrong. It was almost 3:00 a.m and she was in the nurse station. Suddenly, a patient called her, so she left the station with her friend who was also a nurse.

When she was done attending the patient's needs, she happened to pass by the morgue. Angelina noticed that the door was opening and closing on its own. She approched the door and closed it. Just when she was a few steps away from the door, it went open and shut on its own. This time, it's a bit faster.

She quickly walked away and had reached the nurse station. Her nurse friend asked her why she was so pale looking like she has seen a ghost. She said that she just got tired of the patient's demands.

While Angelina was arranging the files, the CCTV security approached her and told her to go to her office because it was urgent. At first, she was confused but when they arrived at the CCTV room; the security showed the footage of her when she was in the morgue. There, the security told her that there was a woman behind her standing by the morgue door and looking at her.

The woman was wearing a white dress with a clean bun. Her height was about 5'4". Angelina had no idea that he was just a few inches away from the woman when she closed the door. Angelina covered her mouth in shock, and chills went down to her spine. She has never been so scared before. She was shaking and even fell from her place.

She asked the CCTV Security to rewind the footage, and the woman was indeed there. The CCTV Security offered her water and calmed her down. She went back to the nurse station and told her friend what happened. It was really a creepy experience.

Angelina thought that this would never happen again, but that day marked the beginning of her creepy experiences. The woman in the morgue began to disturb her in her dreams but every time she woke up, she couldn't describe the face of the woman because it was blurry, and sometimes, she wouldn't turn around.

Sometimes, Angelina would hear whispers in her room. Even in the kitchen, some utensils would just fall on their own. Her parents have noticed the incidents and have noticed that Angelina was so scared. She was already losing weight and couldn't sleep well. Her parents decided to bring her to the hospital, but Angelina refused and told them to bring her to a shaman instead.

She told the Shaman everything, and when the Shaman began her oration, they found out that the ghostly woman was connected to her. The woman never left her, and it was just then when she could finally see and feel her because her third eye has developed. The Shaman also said that the woman has died giving birth to her. Angelina was so confused and when she looked at her father's expression; she knew that her father was afraid and nervous as if he had something to hide.

The Shaman also told Angelina to pray for the woman's soul so that she would find peace. Angelina thanked the Shaman and left. When they got home, she argued with his father, and her father confirmed that it was indeed her mother and what the Shaman said was true. Angelina was so upset and asked her father why he didn't tell her about this, but he just said that it would be best for all of them because Angelina was happy with the mother she knew and loved, he also told her that it was in the past, and he did not want Angelina to worry about it.

Angelina cried in anger and told them that they were unfair and that her life iwas nothing but a big lie. The next day, she went to the Shaman again and told the Shaman to talk with her birth mother. There, she was able to talk with her mother. Her mother communicated through the Shaman. The Shaman told Angelina how proud her mother was because Angelina was able to achieve her dreams, and she has grown up to be beautiful inside and out.

Angelina was crying and apologizing to her. She told her that if she knew that she was dead, she would always pray for her. In the end, the Shaman told her to visit her mother's grave. It seemed that her mother also told the Shaman where her remains were.

Angelina visited her mother's grave and thanked her for choosing her to live and sacrificing her life. She also promised that she will do her best to become a better individual. From that day on, her mother would visit her in her dreams, but she was already smiling. Angelina also mastered her spiritual skills through the help of the Shaman. As for her father and stepmother, she already made peace them.

END OF SUFFERING

Have you ever heard of a miracle baby? Some people have testimonies that they were revived by nurses or even his or her parents have prayed for him or her despite their incapability to have a child.

Mr. and Mrs. Adamson have loved their son Freddie ever since. Freddie had polio, and his wheelchair has always been his best friend. Freddie would always stay in his room looking out from his window. Now that he was already 20 years old, he has learned that his world was already inside his room.

He couldn't change the fact that he loved to play soccer, to run with other people, to take a stroll in parks, and just not to watch the rain pour down and the sun sets from his window. What can he do? Nothing.

For years, he became envious with kids his age and just wished that he has never been born. He became stubborn and would sometimes yell at his nannies whenever they did something wrong. He became mad at simple things like coffee not being tasty like he wanted it to be.

Whenever one of nannies would insist that Freddie should eat but did not want to, he would throw the food onto the floor. There were times as well when he would cry in his room feeling useless, and he would not entertain any person in his room.

There was this time as well where he planned to end his life by slashing his pulse or drinking poison, but thankfully, his nannies were about to bring him food that time and stopped him. He even yelled at them and insisted that he already wanted to end his life because he was useless. He only wanted to end his suffering.

His parents went to his room and confronted him. They told him that he should not think about ending his life because they couldn't bear to lose him. Her mother cried and begged his son to please open up and do not push people away if he had a problem.

Freddie cried and the pain from his voice was evident. His mind was very much in circles. He was stucked between ending his life for him to not feel the pain of being useless and the feeling of being alive because he still wanted to see his parents and live the life that he wanted.

The next day, his parents did not go to work. Instead, they went to the park with Freddie. Freddie enjoyed watching the kids play. One kid approached him and asked him if he could tie his shoes. Freddie nodded and he made the kid happy. Then his father whispered, "You see, Freddie you can still be happy even if you are sitting there."

Freddie smiled at his parents and then continued watching the kids play. Some kids approached Freddie and asked him if he wanted to play with them. Freddie is very much fond of kids so he enjoyed bonding with them. He even opened up with how many times he would dream of seeing himself playing soccer when he was young but he never did that, instead he just watched himself play board games and sit on his wheelchair.

The kids have sympathized with him and told him stories which amazed him. His parents have agreed that Freddie needed to be outside and not locked up because they want to protect him. They also realized that it would be best for Freddie to experience the outside world because it made him happy. So, they informed his nannies to at least allow Freddie to go outside on certain days and certain times.

One day, when one of his nannies went inside the room, she noticed that Freddie was hyperventilating. He was having difficulty in breathing. So she gave him oxygen and called the other nannies to assist her.

Freddie was rushed into the hospital. His parents were very much worried. They stayed there for hours walking back and forth while waiting for the doctor's announcement. When the doctor arrived, he delivered very sad news. He said that he could not revive Freddie anymore because his polio had taken over his whole body.

During Freddie's funeral, one could really feel the melancholic ambiance. It was truly painful to lose your loved one. But in the end, all that his parents could think of was that Freddie's suffering has ended and he was already with the Lord. They were just thankful that they were able to make him happy and to be able to experience parenthood.

TAINTED LIFE

Anna was a girl who was very out-going. She liked to hang out with friends. Since she turned 18 and moved out, her parents lost hold on her. She was free to go anywhere she liked and do anything she desired. She met friends which were not totally good. They would teach her to skip classes and go to places fun like in the bar.

Whenever her parents would call her, she would just lie to them and make excusses like she needed to study, she was in the library, she had school affairs or programs and she cannot hear them nor answer their chats and texts. She learned how to lie to both her family and school. There was a time when she was caught fighting in the corridor with another girl for stealing her boyfriend and plagiarizing her assignments. Indeed, she was trouble.

When her parents heard about this, they immediately cut off her allowance for two months. They even froze Anna's bank account. Anna was so upset and needed to find money for her everyday needs such as food, rent, and other bills; so she consulted and asked her friends to help her. She resorted to prostitution. Sometimes, she would just catcall guys and go with him. After that, she already got enough money for her needs. One of her Johns even got him a car.

At that moment, her desire to buy new clothes and other material things made her crave for more. She then resorted to drug dealing and got addicted to it. She even got arrested for driving under the influence of drugs. She spent her nights drinking and finally got out of school after realizing that her life belonged to the happiness in the outside of the institution.

Her parents tried to stop her. They called her and tried to ask her to come home by personally coming after her, but she just shoved them away and told them that she was happy. She also told them that her friends cared for her more than them because they were there when her parents made her suffer.

Tears fell down from the eyes of her parents and even from Anna's, but they know that it was too late. Her mother swore that Anna would return to her and that she will never be happy. Her father left Anna a glare and turned away.

Few weeks passed and Anna was staying at one of his clients' condominium. His name was Homer and definitely a successful man. He was a CEO of the biggest merchandising company. He was 15 years older than Anna; but Anna did not mind as long she gets what she wants. One morning when she woke up next to Homer, she immediately rushed the comfort room and puked.

She was not feeling well and Homer advised her to go to the doctor by herself because he got meetings to attend and there will be a press conference that day where his company would be featured. Anna was left all alone and the money that Homer gave him for check-up. She went by herself to the hospital by taxi, but on her way there, she fainted. The driver panicked, so he rushed her to the nearest hospital.

Few moments later, she regained consciousness then the doctor arrived. The doctor said that it was normal to faint because she was pregnant. The doctor congratulated her and told her things to take care of her child. Anna was so shocked that she could not even talk. The doctor left, and Anna laid on her bed and cried.

It was a few days when she left the hospital. She cried because Homer did not even visit her. All she could rely on was her friends. At the condo, she heard a knock in the door. The door opened, and she saw Homer. She told Homer everything and argued with him. Homer answered her, but in the end, Homer revealed that he was just there to bid goodbye to Anna.

He couldn't risk his reputation and said that he had nothing to do with the baby. Anna insisted that the baby was his although she was not sure because of the several guys she slept with; she even wants to do a DNA test, but Homer refused and told her that he was done with her. Anna was so devastated and learned to raise the baby alone.

Anna was not happy; she often scolded her daughter and hit her whenever the child would do something wrong she did not mean. One time when she accidentally broke the glass, her mother locked her up in the room, slapped her, and pulled her hair. She even did not let her daughter eat.

She also made her daughter do all the chores everyday and refused to grant her the gift of education. Anna did not know how to live a life anymore. She took drugs and drank alcohol non-stop totally abusing herself and definitely out of direction. One time, she was arrested, and to her surprise, her parents appeared on the visit. They apologized to one another, and both parties were emotional.

Her parents brought Anna to a rehabilitation center, and there, she started a new life and got treated. It is true that you just have to stop abusing yourself and the people around you to finally get the free medication that you need.

WHAT GOES AROUND, COMES AROUND

Brenda was born from a rich family; she could get whatever she wanted. Indeed, she was a spoiled brat. She grew up being the boss in all ways. She always felt like she could always rule the world. Her mother always told her to be kind and never be like her father who has been corrupted with hate in his heart

His father desired all the power. He even resorted to crimes, corruption, and robbery just to gain money and superiority, but the authorities and his victims were not able to get a hold of him because he was so powerful and all his operations were clean and there were not enough evidence.

Brenda tried to follow her mother for being a responsible and respectable woman, but she couldn't just throw her desire for power because she has always been a daddy's girl. Every time that her mother would argue about his father teaching her wrong deeds, most of the time his father would just threaten her mother or even hit her.

Brenda showed no mercy to all of her acts. She has been mean to her classmates. She participated in bullying the nerds and those who had low self-esteem. She would also answer back to her teachers. She was free to not go to school if she didn't want to.

Whenever she would be brought to detention or principal's office, she would be proven not guilty and get out free. For years, Brenda enjoyed the power and freedom. Everyone worshipped or if not, some are afraid to fight her because they knew that whatever happens, she would always win.

When she went to college, she pursued Entrepreneurship. Being the only daughter of her parents, she always wanted to own a company. Her father promised her that she would be the heir; so she was very happy. She studied so hard to earn it, but her attitude never changed. She despised everybody and only cared for herself.

When she was able to acquire her father's company, she did her very best to maintain and impress her father. She was a good director because their sales were increasing. Not until she met her competitor during a business partnership deal in a cafe.

Katherine Mendrez, a wealthy and a successful woman. She was the owner of ten businesses which made Brenda question if she could beat this woman. Brenda was trained and was used to always winning so she fought her fear and courageously mocked Katherine. Katherine just smiled and said that she just realized that education and lavish life couldn't guarantee honor and dignity.

Given the fact that Brenda despises Katherine, for months, they have been competitors. They worked so hard to gain sales. It was an equal distribution of skills and knowledge. Whenever they have a press conference or business events, they would always throw shade at each other and each other's businesses.

Brenda seriously wants to win over Katherine, so she planned to sabotage Katherine's project. She asked one of her trusted conspirators to go to Katherine's office but later on caught on cam by the guard. They tried to escape, but in the end, they were caught. Katherine arrived at the crime scene with her guards. She told her guards not to report what happened but rather she would be the one to talk with the conspirators.

Katherine offered the conspirators more money than Brenda could offer, so they decided to tell Katherine what happened and the person behind the act. Little did they know that they were being filmed by one of Katherine's assistants behind the bush and Katherine also made sure that she secretly recorded their claims.

The next day, Katherine called a press conference and showed the evidence to the people that Brenda sabotaged her. There, she also presented the evidences she gathered from an investigation: evidence that will prove how Brenda and her family were fraud and criminals. As Brenda watched how Katherine was the cause of their downfall, she just cried restlessly and couldn't accept the situation. She just turned off the television and trembled in anger.

Her parents saw what happened and told her to calm down. Indeed, she was very angry and arguments have heated up. When she opened the front door of their house, she saw lots of reporters simultaneously asking random questions regarding their family. The police even presented a warrant of arrest and arrested Brenda and her father.

Few days passed, and Brenda and his father had to suffer the consequences for what they did. Brenda's mother often visited them and the one taking care of the company. However, it was slowly going down because Katherine is doing her best to take it down, and people are more inclined to Katherine's work.

Few days after Katherine visited Brenda and his father in jail, Brenda and his father were so upset that they want to kill her. Katherine just laughed and told them how pathetic they were. Brenda asked her why she would do this to her family and why Katherine always wanted to see them suffer.

Katherine answered, "Because I am the one you bullied in highschool. Who also planned to end her life by overdose. My father went to jail and lost his job because your father made him pay a crime he did not even do. I am Cristina De la Cruz"

Brenda and his father were lost for words and just when they were about to speak, the police shouted that visitation time was over. Katherine left them with a smiling face and a taste of victory. Truly, it was never too late when Karma hits. For Brenda and her family, bad karma hit them, and for Katherine, it's a good karma.

IN THIS HEART

Stella has been miserable ever since she was raped. Her fiancé dumped her when he realized that she was pregnant and that he was not the father. Stella explained that she was raped by her fiancé's best friend, Bryan. Her fiancé was so mad and ended his friendship with Bryan.

Stella raised the child on her own. She left her family because her mother was a drunkard and his father already left them for another woman when she was young. While raising her child, she did not treat him well because it reminded her how bitter her life was. If not because of a free scholarship in their village, her son, James would not be able to go to school.

James was very eager to be able to make his mother proud despite the way he was treated. He could still remember the times when his mother would not show up to his awarding ceremony and the teachers would be the one to put the medal on him. His mother was even absent during Family programs which resulted in him being bullied. For years, he suffered, but he did not tell this to his mother because he didn't want her to worry. He was sure that she wouldn't bother anyway.

If not because of some of his friends and teachers who were there to defend him, he would not survive and might even develop depression. James was very goal-oriented. He knew that if he gave in to his sadness, he would not be able to make his mother proud and happy.

It was also his ultimate goal to ease the pain that his mother was feeling. If he could only just provide her with a bunch of happiness then he would give it to her. Also, whenever he was asked to present his ambitions in class, he would always say that he wanted to be a pilot so that he could bring his mother to another country; show her the joy on the outside, start a new life with her somewhere, and see her smile again.

Stella has always been a drunk, and one time when she went outside at night to gamble, she did not go home early but instead she gambled all day.

James was already used to this, and he learned how to be independent.

The next day when he was preparing for school, Aling Rosa, their neighbor, rushed to James and told him that his mother was found unconscious this morning when she was on her way home. She was a victim of a hit and run and was rushed into the hospital.

James was so worried, so Aling Rosa accompanied James to the hospital. Thankfully, the doctor said that his mother would still survive, but there might be permanent damages like memory loss. A few days passed, James was not able to go to school and stayed with his mother. He just explained to his teacher about his situation.

Everyday, his mother was slowly recovering from the accident. The day came that she woke up and couldn't remember anything at all. She even questioned who James was. As expected, James did not give in. He took care of his mother until they went home.

Suddenly, changes in behavior could be seen because his mother couldn't remember her past anymore. She then learned to love James, and James couldn't ask for anything more. For the first time in forever, his mother learned to express her love for him everyday.

He thanked God for his answered prayer. Truly, his unconditional love for his mother has resulted in him receiving the same from his mother. They lived happily ever after.

TRULY DIVINE

Isabelle has been single for years now. Some of her friends had their own family while others had their special someone already. She is already 32 years old, and had yet find true love.

Isabelle has been praying to meet her soulmate, but to her dismay, nothing was happening. Her friends have her up on many dates but it is always led to disaster. She did not know what to do anymore. She always wanted to have someone who would always stay by her side; who would text her every morning sweet messages, and who would never stop telling her that she was loved every single day.

With that being said, Isabelle couldn't help herself but be bitter to see kissing couples whenever she walked around. Couples who were happily snuggling on benches made her wish even more that she had someone special.

Every time she would attend the wedding of her friends, she would always participate in the bouquet throwing, and most of the time, she would be lucky to catch the bouquet; unfortunately until now, she never had someone. She seriously thought that it was just a silly superstition or just something to make the visitors entertained.

More so, there was this time when she really liked someone and she tried to flirt with him. They dated for three months. It was a happy and healthy relationship until that candle light dinner they had in a fancy restaurant. The man admitted that he was having homosexual tendencies and that he has been eyeing for someone.

Isabelle could not believe what happened. All she could do was cry and chase away the man that she loved and broke her heart. Even though it was just three months, she had felt that she has a purpose. Thankfully her parents were there to comfort her and to fix her mascara.

Her only best friend and who was also getting married in a few months was her sister Jen.

She always told Isabelle that she would find the right man for her in God's perfect timing, but Isabelle just couldn't wait any longer. She was really longing for true love.

One time when she went to church with her family, she happened to stumble with a nun. It was sister Gilda and she has been a nun for 10 years now. Having the attitude of being talkative, Jen has opened up that Isabelle cannot find a soulmate. Isabelle tried to stop Jen, but it was too late. Sister Gilda already laughed kindly.

Sister Gilda told her she that should not lose hope and that God had a purpose on everything that she was going through. God was the only way for happiness and that she should not depend it on a single person. She also told Isabelle that she could be happy if she chose to be. She also opened up the possibility that maybe God was preparing her for something special, can be a breakthrough which was why she couldn't love and be ready for something big at the same time.

A year later, Isabelle and Sister Gilda became good friends. Isabelle would often volunteer to charity and church outreach programs. There, she found her new purpose. She was very much delighted to help people and seeing the smile on their faces motivated her about everything that she did.

During her speeches on one of her outreach programs, she opened up that it was not long since she was longing for love, but now she already found out her real purpose and that was to help those who were in need and be God's servant. Sister Gilda and other church coordinators clapped their hands and almost shed a tear when they heard Isabelle's speech.

From that day on, Sister Gilda saw Isabelle's crucible and that she was also happy to see that she made her stronger and content on what she had. Years passed, Isabelle continued serving the Church, and it was not long since she told her family that she wanted to continue helping people and serving God. She wanted to be divine and become closer to God. It turned out that she loves being His servant.

The only way she could achieve her aspiration was by strengthening her faith even more. She revealed that she wanted to be a nun. At first, her family was shocked but proud. Isabelle then talked about how she realized why all of her dates and relationships were a disaster, it was because she was destined to serve God for the rest of her life.

In a few days, Isabelle went to the convent and pursued being a nun. She went into a divination. She had been there for years until the day when her family visited her. Her niece kissed her hand, and when they asked each other about their lives, Isabelle was completely happy.

HEART TO ACCEPT

Cathy was the type of girl who any girl would want to be. Some did not know why she was so lucky. Aside from the beauty and an hourglass body, she was also that type of woman who knew how to handle things very well. Some say that her parents were very lucky to have her as a daughter.

Being famous has never been easy because Cathy had no time for herself. Having 19 million followers on Instagram and being at school makde it a hassle for her. She needed to ignore everything just for her to eat quietly or even relax.

She had this mean attitude, for she knew that she has already distant from the people around her. Some people would approach her, and she would just roll her eyes. Even her friends would be silent whenever she would rant about something. Most of the time, they would suggest, but if Cathy does not agree, all that they will receive was an insult or a rolling eyes. How lucky she was because she still had friends.

However, something was strange. Others were already asking why she never flaunted her boyfriend on social media. They were always wondering if she ever had one. Whenever she was being interviewed about it, she would just smile and would say that she would rather keep her love life private.

How long could she keep this private? This day was just a normal day she thought, but then she received a text from an unknown number telling her to meet him at a secret hideout in the middle of the night. She called the number when she went home from school, and she recognized his voice. It was Sid, one of his friends.

If you were wondering why she was able to escape the paparazzi and everyone, well she already mastered the act of escaping the media. She already knew her way towards being unseen.

When she went to Sid's house, it turned out that he was not just a friend. They had an affair. Sid was not just a typical guy who was similar with her age. He was 30 years older than her. It turned out that he was no longer satisfied with his wife because she was already old as well.

Before Cathy left Sid's house, Sid gave her jewelry worth 500,000 php. He even bought her Louis Vuitton bags and branded clothes. You could really see how happy she was. She thanked Sid by kissing him on the lips but then Sid's phone rang; it was his wife coming home from work.

Sid bid goodbye to her Cathy. When she got home, Cathy saw her mother coughing and very pale. She immediately gave her medicine. Cathy has loved her mother ever since her father died due to cancer. From that day on, she would do her best to gain wealth so that she can provide her mother all the things that she wanted.

Cathy's mother refused to have her daughter do all the work although she was getting weaker by the day. Cathy insisted because she knew she had to work very hard for their daily needs; moreover, she already loved being popular and being the it girl.

One day when she got out of class, a woman went to her school pulled her hair and insulted her. Cathy fought back because she didn't even know the woman. She had no idea whatever the woman was raging about.

Cathy looked everywhere to see people gathering around them. Some were gossiping about them while others were handling their phones taking pictures and videos about them. The woman wearing a green sleeve dress and 2 inch black heels revealed that she was the wife of Sid and that she knew about their affair.

Everybody was shocked. Cathy tried to deny it, but then Sid's wife threw pictures of her with Sid. It turned out that she hired an investigator because she could sense that something was off with Sid lately. She also revealed that the reason why Cathy has become popular was that she was flirting with directors and producers.

From that day on, Cathy's reputation has gone bad. She was still the most popular girl in school. She became the talk of the town but all she could hear was insult. She could do nothing but accept the fact that she was just a trash in everybody's eyes. She wanted to do something to regain her good image but she was forced to accept the fact that people had no sympathy for her anymore.

If only she accepted her simple life and that she could be happy living with her mother then she would never experience this kind of humiliation. If only she did not crave for power and fame, her life would never be upside down. Now, she realized that she would never be happy longing for fame, power, and material things.

For years, she has suffered the stares of people. Stares which she knew were already killing her. Gossips about her that she learned to shrug off have increased, but she was determined to move on. During their Prom Night, she stood up on stage and apologized to everybody for being mean and for being so stubborn.

She said that she has learned from her mistakes and that she was done punishing herself from the mistakes she made. She also included in her tearful speech that she already accepted her mistakes for it was a part of her now and that she already accepted who she was.

Tag-ulan sa Kaarawan ni Juan

"Hayaan mong bahagyang magsayaw ang buhay sa mga hangganan ng panahon na parang hamog sa dulo ng dahon."
—Rabindranath Tagore

***

Ang mga akda sa kabanatang ito ay kuha sa mga piling *journal* at *literary notebook* na naisulat ng manunulat noong nasa ika-pito hanggang ika-siyam na gulang pa lamang ito at noo'y nasa antas tersyarya. Sa panahon ding iyon siya nagsimulang magsanay sumulat ng iba't ibang akdang pampanitikan sa wikang Filipino at Ingles. Upang mapanatili ang noong diskarte at istilo sa pagsulat ng may akda. Hiniling nito na huwag galawin, baguhin o palitan ang ano mang bahagi ng orihinal niyang piyesa. Samakatuwid, ang piling dagli at maikling kwento na inyong mababasa ay hango mismo sa orihinal na katha at nailimbag na hindi dumaan sa masusing pagsusuri.

SAKIT AT PAGMAMAHAL

Sa baryo ng Sasoba, isang lalaki na nagngangalang Juan ang madalas pag-usapan ng mga tao. Maliban kasi sa pagiging lasingero nito, madalas pa niyang saktan ang kanyang mag-ina tuwing ito'y uuwi galing inuman. Araw-araw siya kung mag-inom, at sa tuwing uuwi siya, dinig na dinig hanggang kapit-bahay ang sigaw at pagwawala nito. Kaya naman alam na alam na ng mga kapit-bahay pag nakauwi na ito. Kalampag dito, sigaw doon, at ano-ano pang pag iingay ang ginagawa nito.

Nakalulungkot lang marinig na dumaragdag pa sa ingay itong anak niya at asawa na nagmamakaawang huwag silang galawin at saktan. Ngunit ugali na talaga ni Juan ang gawing *punching bag* ang mag-ina niya sa tuwing uuwi siya. Suntok dito, tandyak doon, at kung ano-ano pang pananakit ang ginagawa nito sa kanila. Hihinto lamang ito kapag dinalaw na siya ng antok at makatulog sa pagod sa pambubugbog. Kaya naman itong asawa niya na si Maria, ay madalas ipatago sa kapit-bahay niyang si Aling Nena ang anak kapag alam nitong pauwi na ang asawa.

"Tao po! Tao po, Aling Nena. Nariyan po ba kayo?" nagmamadaling katok ni Maria sa pintuan nila Aling Nena habang bitbit-bitbit ang sampung taong gulang niyang anak na si Cecille.

Dali-dali namang binuksan ni Aling Nena ang pintuan niya habang lumilingon-lingon sa paligid ng daan. "Andyan na ba siya? Naku, e kung pumasok ka na rin kaya dito? Nag-aalala ako sayo Maria. " Wika nito habang hawak ang kamay ni Maria.

"Hindi ho pwede Aling Nena, Alam niyo naman po si Juan, hahanapin at hahanapin ako nun. Heto po si Cecille, alam niyo na po ang gagawin ha. Pasensya na po sa abala Aling Nena ha. Araw-araw nalang ganito. Maraming salamat po sa tulong ninyo." Mangiyak-ngiyak na sabi ni Maria habang pinapapasok si Cecille sa loob ng bahay nila Aling Nena.

"O anak Cecille, mag pakabait ka dyan ha? Wag mo pasasakitin ang ulo ni Aling Nena. Kukuhanin din kita maya-maya pag tulog na ang itay mo." Bilin ni Maria kay Cecille habang nagmamadali umalis.

Nang makaalis na ito ay sakto namang papasok ng gate si Juan habang nagsisisigaw sa labas. Agad sinara ni Aling Nena ang pintuan niya. Dito ay inalalayan na ni Maria si Juan papasok sa kanilang tahanan habang nakatingin sa pintuan nila Aling Nena.

"Hoy babae? Nasaan ang anak mo?" lango at iika-ikang nitong tanong habang inaakbayan siya ni Maria papasok ng bahay.

"Wala ang anak mo, nasa pinsan niya sa kabilang kanto." Wika ni Maria habang iniuupo siya sa may sala.

"Putang-ina mo kang babae ka! 'Wag mo kong pinaglololokong hayop ka! Nasaan ang malandi mong anak!" sigaw nito habang nanlilisik ang tingin kay Maria.

"Tama na Juan, ako nalang ang saktan mo. Huwag mo ng idamay ang anak mo." Pagmamaka-awa ni Maria.

Nagsimula na itong magwala at magtatatalak. Dinig na dinig ni Aling Nena sa kabilang bahay ang nangyayari. Kaya naman inakyat niya si Cecille sa kwarto at binilinan na kahit anong mangyari ay huwag na huwag itong lalabas. Siya namang tango ng bata. Sa pagkakataong ito ay hindi na nakatiis si Aling Nena. Lumabas siya upang puntahan at pasukin si Maria at Juan sa kanilang bahay. Kitang-kita ni Aling Nena kung paano bunuin ni Juan at pagtatadyakan si Maria na ikinalupaypay nito sa sahig. Hinila ni Aling Nena si Juan papalayo.

"Hoy Juan! Ano ba? Buong buhay mo na lang bang sasaktan itong mag-ina mo. Walang hiya ka! Naturingan ka pa man ding retiradong pulis, pero daig mo pa ang kriminal kung pagbuhatan ng kamay ang mag-ina mo" Pasigaw na sabi ni Aling Nena habang itinatayo si Maria.

"Hoy ikaw matanda ka! Huwag kang makielam sa buhay ng may buhay! Away namin mag-asawa ito! Kaya umalis-alis ka sa harapan ko! Baka hindi ako makapag-pigil sa'yo at pati ikaw masaktan ko! Kahit patayin ko ang mag-ina ko, wala ka na doon! Kaya Alis! Alis!" Sigaw ni Juan kay Aling Nena ng may pambabastos.

"Bastos ka talagang lalaki ka! Hindi mo na ako ginalang bilang matanda!" Wika ni Aling Nena habang hinahampas-hampas nito sa balikat si Juan.

Hindi na nga nakapag-pigil at sinampal na ni Juan si Aling Nena na ikinatumba nito, kagyat na sana nitong bubunutin ang kanyang baril sa kaliwang bulsa, ngunit agad siyang pinukpok ng bote sa ulo ni Maria dahilan upang mabitawan niya ito. Agad namang itinayo ni Maria si Aling Nena at itinulak palabas ng bahay saka nito ikinandado ang pinto upang hindi na muling makapasok ang matanda

"Buksan mo ang pinto Maria! Lumabas ka dyan! Layasan mo na yang asawa mong kampon ni Satanas!" Mangiyak-ngiyak na sigaw ni Aling Nena.

Nagumpisa nang mangatok ang matanda sa pintuan ng mga kalapit-bahay nito upang humingi ng tulong. Kaya naman halos lahat ay naantala sa kanilang pagkakahimbing dala ng paghagulgol niya habang nangangalampag sa pintuan. Ilang segundo pa'y nakarinig sila ng tatlong putok ng baril na nanggaling sa bahay nila Maria at Juan. Narinig ito ng lahat pati na ni Cecille. Kaya naman dali-dali itong lumabas sa bahay nila Aling Nena at tumakbo pauwi sa kanila. At doon tumambad ang malamig at duguang katawan ng kanyang ama.

"Tay!" Sigaw ni Cecille habang umiiyak at yakap-yakap ang nakahandusay na katawan ni Juan.

Agad na pumasok si Aling Nena sa loob ng bahay upang kuhanin ang baril sa kamay ni Maria. Habang yakap-yakap niya ito ay maririnig ang tunog ng sirena ng pulis. Nang makarating ang mga pulis ay agad na nilang pinosasan si Maria at dinala sa istasyon nila upang siyasatin sa mga nangyari.

Hinatulan ng sampung-taong pagkakakulong si Maria sa salang pag-patay kay Juan. Masakit mang mawalay sa anak niyang si Cecille, tinanggap pa rin niya ito ng maluwag sa kaniyang puso.

Ilang taon na rin ang lumipas ng pumanaw ang ama ni Cecille. Si Aling Nena na rin ang pansamantalang kumupkop sa kanya buhat ng makulong si Maria. Ilang taon na rin siyang naghihintay sa parole ng ina. Madalas rin niyang ma-miss ang ama kahit pa sinasaktan silang mag-ina noon. Sa huli, namayani pa rin ang pagmamahal sa puso ni Cecille.

"Kaunting hintay nalang, at makakalaya na ang iyong ina Cecille. Magkakasama na rin kayo." Nakangiting sabi ni Aling Nena habang niyayakap siya nito.

BULAKLAK NG KAHAPON

Taon-taon simula nang mag-kinse anyos ako ay nakatatanggap na ako ng isang bungkos ng mga bulaklak sa isang hindi kilalang tao. Kaya palaisipan sa amin nila Papa at Mama kung sino ba ang estranghero na taon-taon kung makapag-padala ng ng bulaklak sa aking kaarawan.

"Happy birthday to you... Happy birthday to you... Happy birthday dear Princess... Happy birthday to you" Kanta nila Mama at Papa habang hawak-hawak papunta sa akin ang isang napakaganda at tiyak kong napakasarap na Cake.

"Happy 26th birthday Princess anak!" bati ni Papa sa akin nang nakangiti habang hawak ang Cake.

"Mag-wish ka muna bago mo ihipan yang kandila anak. Masayang-masaya kami ng Papa mo para sa iyo." Wika ni Mama na mangiyak-ngiyak habang niyayakap ako.

Sa oras na iyon ay pumikit ako upang humiling. Dalawa lang naman ang aking hiling tuwing birthday ko. Ang maging safe kami lagi nila Mama at Papa at malaman kung sino ang nagpapadala ng bulaklak sa akin taon-taon.

Ilang sigundo pa ay binuksan ko na ang aking mga mata at inihipan ang Cake. Nang sandaling iyon ay masayang-masaya akong hinalikan nila Papa at Mama. Agad naman akong naiyak sa tuwa dahil kahit papaano ay naalala nilang ipaghanda at bilhan ako ng Cake.

Sabay-sabay naming pinagsaluhan ang inihanda na pagkain ni Mama para sa akin. Habang kumakain ay biglang nagsalita si Papa at nagtanong...

"Siya nga pala anak, kailan niyo ba balak magpakasal ni Ferdie? Naku anak, pina-aalalahanan lang kita ha, lalo na at nagkaka-edad kana." Sabi ni Papa habang iniaabot ang ulam kay Mama.

"Sa susunod po na taon Pa, Napag-usapan na rin namin ni Ferdie ang tungkol doon.

Pagkatapos ng kasal, balak namin ni Ferdie na mamuhay sa US at doon na mag-buntis at manganak Pa." Wika ko ng medyo nasasabik.

"Naku, 'wag mo namang madaliin ang anak mo. Hayaan mo siyang magdesisyon para sa sarili niya. Andito pa naman tayo. Hanggat gusto mo pa dito Princess anak. Okay lang sa amin ng Papa mo." Sabi ni Mama na medyo iritable kay Papa.

"Mama naman, diba nag-usap na tayo tungkol dito. Desidido na talaga kami ni Ferdie magpakasal sa susunod na taon." Paunawa kong sabi kay Mama.

Nang mga sandaling iyon, natahimik si Mama. At napansin namin ni Papa na medyo maluha-luha ito. Kaya naman agad siyang niyakap at kinausap ni Papa.

"Ma, 'wag ka namang ganyan. Pati tuloy ako nalulungkot sa ginagawa mo. Alam kong mahirap pero kailangan nating tangapin na hihiwalay at hihiwalay itong nag-iisa nating anak." Wika ni Papa habang yakap-yakap si Mama.

"Okay lang ako. Naluluha ako dahil masaya ako para sa anak natin. Hindi ko lang talaga maiwasang malungkot pag naiisip ko na aalis si Princess at iiwan na niya tayo." Wika ni Mama na mas lalo pang umiyak.

Hindi ko na rin napigilang maiyak nang sandaling iyon at niyakap si Mama.

"Mama, maraming salamat sa lahat-lahat. Naku, dadalaw naman ako dito sa inyo. At huwag ka mag-alala, dadalasan namin ang pag-dalaw ni Ferdie." Sabi ko habang yakap-yakap si Mama.

"Naku, ano ba yan. Birthday na birthday mo nag-iiyakan tayo. Basta anak masaya ako para sa'yo at mahal na mahal ka namin ng Papa mo." Wika ni Mama habang nakangiti at pinupunasan ang luha gamit ang kanyang damit.

Nang matapos kaming kumain, inumpisahan na ni Mama hiwain ang Cake na bi-nake niya upang matikman namin ni Papa. Maya-maya pa ay may nag-door bell sa gate.

"Tao po. Andyan po ba si Princes Cruz? May padala po para sa kanya." Sigaw ng Delivery Boy.

"Oo, heto na. Sandali lang." Sigaw ko naman habang palabas ng bahay.

"Maam, heto po yung bulaklak na padala sa inyo. Happy birthday po. Ang tanda niyo na po" Sabi niya habang nakangisi.

"Naku, salamat Kuya. Medyo nanaba ka ha. Taon-taon na lang at nagkikita tayo para lang sa bulaklak na ito. Wala ka pa rin bang alam kung kanino ito galing?" Bati ko ng tumatawa.

"Naku Ma'am. Negative tayo dyan. Kung alam ko lang po ay dati pa noong kinse anyos kayo ay sinabi ko na. Kaso wala po talaga e." Pakamot-kamot nitong sabi.

"Oo na Kuya. Naku, baka gusto mo muna pumasok sandali, may pagkain sa loob. Tara sa loob!" Madali kong sabi.

"Salamat na lang po Ma'am. Marami pa po akong ide-deliver e. Happy birthday na lang po." Nakangiti niyang sabi.

"Ganun ba. Sandali lang Kuya, Heto dalhin mo na lang itong sandwich. Kainin mo mamaya pag nagutom ka." Sabi ko habang ibinibigay ang sandwich sa kanya.

"Sige po Ma'am. Maraming salamat po. See you next year po." Pabiro nitong sabi habang papaalis.

"Che! Sige na. Alis na!" Dagdag ko.

Nang matanggap ang bulaklak ay agad ko ito ipinakita kina Mama at Papa. Hindi na sila nagtanong kung kanino galing ito.

"Ma, Pa. Look! Mga bulaklak nanaman. Kanino ba talaga nanggagaling ang mga ito. Sa hinaba-haba ng panahon, hindi pa ba siya nagsasawang bigyan ako ng bulaklak?" Sabi ko habang inaamoy-amoy ito.

"Baka naman 'nak meron kang nagawang mabuti sa isang tao, kaya hindi ka malimutan nito. At taon-taon na lang kung pasalamatan ka." Sagot ni Mama

"Meron sigurong isang tao na mahal na mahal ka at hindi ka kayang kalimutan, kaya ganun na lang kung padalhan ka ng mga bulaklak taon-taon." Dagdag pa ni Papa.

Binali-wala ko na lang ang mga sinabing nilang 'yun. Kahit pa gaano kong isipin, wala akong tao na tinulungan at natulungan noong bata ako.

Dis-oras na ng gabi ay gising pa ako, nakatitig sa mga bulaklak na aking natanggap nitong hapon lang. Naantala ang aking pagkatulala sa mga ito nang biglang may kumatok sa pintuan. Nang magbukas ito, nakita ko si Mama na may dala-dalang gatas.

"Hating-gabi na ha. Hindi ka pa inaantok? Heto, tinimplahan kita ng maligamgam na gatas. Inumin mo muna nang makatulog ka na." Wika nito habang inilalagay sa may maliit na lamesa sa tabi ng higaan ko ang isang-basong gatas.

"Ano't hindi ka pa tulog? Ano bang iniisip mo? Hindi maganda sa kalusugan yang pagpupuyat, naku. Baka hagipin ka ng sakit niyan." Dagdag pa niya.

"Wala naman po Ma. Hindi lang talaga ako makatulog. Napadami kasi ako ng Cake kanina. Ang sarap po ng luto nyo Mama." Sabi ko ng nakangiti sa kanya.

"Naku, nambola ka pa. Halika nga dito. Payakap ako sa anak kong maganda." Sabi ni Mama habang niyayakap ako.

"Ma. Natandaan mo dati noong nag-aaral ako sa elementarya madalas mo akong padalhan ng pagkarami-raming pagkain sa bag. Pero nauubos ko 'yun Ma kasi ang sarap mo magluto. Kaso nga lang araw-araw padagdag ng padagdag mga pinadadala mo sa akin. Kaya naman ang taba-taba ko ng mga panahong 'yun." Sabi ko habang nakahiga sa kanlungan niya.

"Talaga lang ha. Kaya pala ipinamimigay mo ang baon mong pagkain sa mga kaklasi mong walang baon." Wika ni Mama ng nakatawa.

"Kanino nyo naman nalaman 'yun Ma" Kabado kong tanong.

"Naku, papunta ka pa lang. Pabalik na ako. Isang araw nakita kita sa may Canteen. Pinamimigay mo ang pagkain na niluto ko sa mga kaklasi mong walang baon. Kaya naman dinadamihan ko araw-araw ang baon mo kasi alam ko ishe-share mo 'yun sa mga kaklasi mo." Tumatawang sabi ni Mama.

"Ma, sorry ha. Hindi naman sa ayaw ko ang mga luto mo dati. Kaso nga lang naaawa ako sa mga kaklasi ko na walang baon. Nung mga panahong iyon, since marami naman, ipinamigay ko 'yung iba." Pangangatuwiran kong sabi kay Mama.

"Naku, anak okay lang 'yun. Mabuti lang ang ginawa mo. Sa mga bagay na ganun ay nakatulung ka sa kapwa mo. 'Yun ang mahalaga." Wika ni Mama habang hinahaplos-haplos ang ulo ko.

"Mana lang po ako sa inyo Ma. Napakabait at napaka-matulungin nyo rin po. Salamat po sa pag-aaruga sa akin." Sabi ko habang mahigpit na niyayakap ang bewang ni Mama.

"Naku, o sya na. Matulog ka na dyan at maaga pa ang pasok mo sa trabaho bukas. Siya nga pala nagkita kami ng Ninang mo kanina. Ipache-check up daw niya ang apo nito sa'yo bukas. Sabi ko agahan niya sa klinika mo." Pahabol na sabi ni Mama

"Okay Ma. No problem po. Good night Mama." Wika ko habang nakahiga at nakangiti sa kanya.

"Good night sa maganda at mambobola kong anak." Sabi niya palabas ng kwarto.

Kinabukasan habang nasa klinika ako. May tumawag sa landline at agad namang sinagot ito ng Nurse Aide.

"Excuse me Doc, Mama nyo po nasa landline." Sabi ng Nurse Aide.

"Paki-sabi tinatapos ko lang itong mga nagpapa-check up. Ako na lang tatawag sa kanya maya-maya." Habilin ko sa Nurse.

Nang matapos kong icheck-up ang mga pasyente ay nagpahinga muna ako ng ilang minuto at uminom ng mainit na kape. Habang umiinom at nagpapahinga sa loob ng kwarto, napatingin ako sa isang figurine na bigay ni Papa na naka-display sa may lamesa ko. Dun at naalala ko na tatawagan ko nga pala si Mama. Pumunta ako sa may telepono at tumawag sa bahay upang malaman kung bakit napatawag si Mama.

"Hello Ma? Kamusta dyan? Ba't napatawag ka kanina?" Tanong ko sa kanya.

"Princess ang Papa mo..." Sagot ni Mama habang humahagulgol ng iyak.

Bigla kong binaba ang telepono at inayos ang gamit ko. Dali-dali akong umalis ng klinika at hinarurot ang kotse ko pauwe. Nang makarating sa bahay tumambad sa akin ang walang buhay nang katawan ni Papa.

"Papa..." Hagulgol ko habang yakap-yakap ito.

Hindi ko alam ang gagawin ng mga oras na iyon. Iniwan na ako ng isa sa mga mahahalagang tao sa buhay ko. Napaluhod na lamang ako sa sakit ng makita si Papa na wala nang buhay sa may sala. Agad kong tinanong si Mama kung anong nangyari, hindi rin siya makausap ng maayos dala ng paghikbi nito habang umiiyak. Sinabi ni Ninang na inatake sa puso ang Papa habang nakaupo sa sala.

Bumaha ang mga luha sa burol ni Papa. Dumating ang mga kamag-anak namin galing sa iba't ibang lugar upang makiramay. Kami naman ni Mama ay halos mamatay sa kaiiyak at pagdadalamhati. Kaya naman si Ninang na muna ang umasikaso sa lahat. Hindi namin iniwan ni Mama si Papa hanggang sa huling hantungan nito.

Ilang araw pa ang lumipas nang mawala si Papa ay mas lalo pang tumindi ang sakit na nadarama namin ni Mama. Hanggang si Mama ay dumaan sa matinding depresyon na nagdulot ng iba't ibang sakit sa kaniyang katawan. Ako nama'y tumigil muna sa pagta-trabaho upang bantayan si Mama.

Dumaan ang ilang buwan ay medyo bumuti-buti na rin ang lagay ni Mama. Ngunit madalas pa rin itong tulala at wala sa sarili. Kaya naman hinanapan ko ito ng Nurse na magbabantay sa kanya at sa kalusugan nito. Kahit masakit, unti-unti ko nang natatanggap ang pagkawala ni Papa.

Dumaan ang ilang mga taon mula nang pumanaw si Papa. Masaya naming ipinagpatuloy ni Mama ang buhay.

"Happy birthday to you...Happy birthday to you...Happy birthday dear Princess... Happy birthday to you." Kanta ni Mama habang hawak ang bi-nake nitong Cake.

Pumikit ako upang mag-wish. Ngunit bago pa ako makapag-wish ay biglang tunog nanaman ng door bell na dahilan upang muli nanaman akong lumabas.

"Ma'am. Happy birthday po. Heto ang bulaklak niyo." Nakangiti nanamang sabi ni Kuya

"Salamat po Kuya. Heto po ang pagkain. Kainin niyo po tapos niyo mag-deliver. Hindi ko na po kayo aayahin pumasok, siguradong tatanggihan nyo nanaman po ako." Sabi ko ng nakangiti sa kanya.

"Mukhang 'di po yata kayo masaya sa birthday nyo ngayon ha. Napansin ko po iyon ilang taon na rin ang nakakaraan na medyo malungkot kayo sa mga birthday nyo." Wika nito ng may pag-uusisa

"Naku, Kuya. Hindi po. Masaya po ako. Hindi nga lang ganun ka saya, kasi ilang taon na rin na wala si Papa sa birthday ko." Napayuko kong sabi.

"Naku, Ma'am. Kung nasaan man ang Papa nyo ngayon, tiyak na masaya 'yun." Pataas-taas kilay niyang sabi.

"Salamat Kuya. Ingat po kayo." Nag-aalala kong sabi.

"Kayo 'din po Ma'am. Hiling ko maging masaya na kayo." Wika ni Kuya

Pagpasok ko sa loob, kita ni Mama ang ngiti ko at ang bulaklak na hawak ko. Agad naman itong nagsalita.

"Sandali lang, hindi mo pa naiihipan itong Cake mo." Sabi niya habang hawak ang Cake.

Agad naman akong pumikit upang mag-wish. Sa pagkakataong ito, tatlo na ang kahilingan ko. Una, ang mas lalo pang pagbuti ni Mama. Ikalawa, kung nasaan man si Papa ngayon, nawa'y maging masaya siya at ang ikatlo, syempre gusto ko na talaga malaman kung sino ang nagbibigay ng bulaklak sa akin taon-taon.

Sabay namin dalawa ni Mama pinagsaluhan ang luto niya habang naguusap.

"Ilang taon na rin wala si Papa. Kamusta na kaya siya?" Tanong ko habang ipinaiikot-ikot ang tinidor sa lutong spaghetti ni Mama

"Alam kong masaya siya habang nakikita tayo. Mahal na mahal tayo ng Papa mo anak. Alam ko saan man tayo magpunta, binabantayan niya tayo." Nakangiting niyang sabi..

Ilang buwan ang lumipas at minabuti na namin ni Ferdie ang magpakasal. Sa isang simbahan kung saan kami madalas magsimba nila Mama at Papa. Maluha-luha si Mama nang makita niya akong naka traje be boda at lumalakad papuntang altar.

Makikita sa mata ni Mama ang lubos na kasiyahan lalo na nang matapos ang kasal ay tumuloy muna kami sa isang napakanda at napagarang hotel na pagmamay-ari ng asawa ko.

"Masayang-masaya ako anak, sa wakas ay ikinasal ka na. Bubuo ka na ng sarili mong pamilya. Huwag na huwag mong kalilimutan ang mga payo namin ng Papa mo sa'yo ha. Alam kong magiging mabuti kang ina sa mga anak mo. Kasi mabait ka. Mahal na mahal kita anak." Umiiyak na sabi ni Mama.

"Opo Ma. Lahat ng mga payo nyo. Babaunin ko lahat iyon pati na sa aking pag-tanda. Maraming salamat po sa inyo ni Papa. Kahit ampon niyo lamang ako, tinuring nyo pa rin akong parang tunay nyong anak. Mahal na mahal ko po kayo Mama. Hinding-hindi po ako makakalimot kailanman." Hagulgol kong sagot sa kanya habang niyayakap siya.

Isang taon matapos ang aking kasal. Pumanaw si Mama sa sakit niyang diabetes. Iyon din ang taon na huminto sa pagdating ang bungkos ng mga bulaklak sa aking kaarawan.

"Ang pag-abot sa iyong mga pangarap
ang pinakamalaking abentura ng buhay."
— Oprah Winfrey

WHO IS JOMARI PANGILINAN?

People who know Jomari Paulino Pangilinan would describe him as a passionate person. He pursues a variety of fields and manifests both passion and potential in most of them: truly a born artist who aspires to be many things in life.

Jomari Paulino is a secondary school English educator and a graduate of Don Honorio Ventura Technological State University. He spent the early years of his teaching career rendering service at Assumpta Technical High School and the University of the Assumption. Currently, he is employed under the Department of Education making a difference at Pandaras Integrated School.

At an early age, Jomari Paulino has exhibited exemplary promise in the field of writing. He won several journalism awards both in elementary and in high school which earned him the title "Journalist of the Year" upon his graduation. He also gained a number of recognitions in his teaching career including the Classroom Superhero (Outstanding Teacher Award), First-Placer in the Creative Writing Contest, First-Placer in the Storybook Writing Contest, First-Placer in the Photo Contest, and Second-Placer in the Digitized Storytelling Contest.

A jack of all trades is a master of none but always better than a master of one. Aside from being a gifted writer and a dedicated educator, Jomari Paulino also excels in the arts: drawing, photography, videography, theater, event organizing, voice-acting, and music. Since high school, he has produced and directed several local theatrical plays and musicals which delighted audience from different walks of life.

In college, he was a renowned disk jockey (DJ) at the university's local radio station and the founder of the collegiate glee club. He was also a volunteer for the University Student Council, and although he never had the initiative to lead the university, he ensured the fairness in the selection of student leaders by being the general secretary for the

Student Commission of Elections two years in a row.

As a teacher, Jomari Paulino did not stop sharing his talents. Aside from being in the core group of the division's English teachers and being well-loved by students and colleagues alike, he had the opportunity to coach students into victory among the following categories: extemporaneous speech, speech choir, dramatic monologue, scriptwriting and radio broadcasting, feature writing, editorial cartooning, headline writing and copyreading, and photojournalism.

Whatever he does, he does it with heart and a hundred percent dedication. Jomari Paulino is innovative, creative, and bright. He learns from his mistakes and rise to the top. Being many things may sound difficult, and it is; however, St. Teresa of Calcutta once said that not all people can do great things, but we can do small things with great love.

Facebook: Jopao Pangilinan

E-mail: jom2625@gmail.com

OTHER BOOKS BY EDISON DIZON

SHADES OF SEASONS: Soulful Autumn

SHADES OF SEASONS: Cold Dark Winter's Night

SHADES OF SEASONS: Endless Spring

SHADES OF SEASONS: Summertime Blues

ISANG TASA NG TSAA PARA SA'YO: Tula at Prosa

THE VOICE WITHIN MY SOUL

TAG-ULAN SA KAARAWAN NI JUAN: Dagli at Maikling Kwento

THE SOUL SENTIMENTS: NO BLAMES FOR THIS PAIN

THE SOUL SENTIMENTS: LIKE LAST NIGHT NEVER HAPPENED